D0554401

DEAD
RUN

DEAD RUN

An Inspector Heimrich Mystery

by

Richard Lockridge

J. B. Lippincott Company
New York and Philadelphia

for Hildy

DEAD
RUN

Chapter 1

INSPECTOR M. L. HEIMRICH, Bureau of Criminal Investigation, New York State Police, walked out of the barracks of Troop K in Washington Hollow to its parking lot. It was raining, more resolutely than the United States Weather Service had expected. The weather service had contemplated partial cloudiness, with a chance of showers, and continued mild temperatures, turning colder late in the day. The pressure systems had not, apparently, been listening, at least not intently. Well, not much can be expected of the weather on the twenty-third of December.

It was not only wet as Heimrich walked across the lot to his car. It was also cold. He had checked the temperature before he left the office. Thirty-five it had been then. At a little after noon it had been thirty-eight and partly cloudy. Still, it could have been worse. At the latitude of Washington Hollow, it usually was at this time of year. Often, in late December, snow lay heavy in mid-New York state.

As he got into the Buick with its excessively long radio antenna, Heimrich looked up at a nearby tree. The light from the overhead floods reached it. The bare twigs glistened wet in the light. Water dripped from them, which was consoling. Of course, the temperature usually dropped after sundown. But the weather service had predicted an overnight low in the upper thirties. (It had also, of course, forecast a chance of "showers." Rain had started falling around three in the afternoon and continued to fall. Weather Service could call that a shower if it wanted to.)

The engine caught at the first try. Heimrich turned the heater up and cold air blew from the vents. He should, of course, have worn a heavier coat. Put not your trust in meteorologists. But the car would warm up when the engine did. And at home Susan would have the fire going. Perhaps Michael and his friend had already got to Van Brunt. Quite a drive down from Hanover, New Hampshire, but not too long a trip the way kids drove. And, while the snow was a couple of feet deep in Hanover, the roads were clear. Michael had assured his mother of that when he called the night before.

His call had been a pleasant surprise for Susan. Michael had not expected to make it home for this Christmas. The junk heap would never make it, he had written them a week earlier. He might try to make it to Boston. He might just stay in Hanover and try to do something about his skiing, which remained lousy. "But you both have a fine Christmas."

But then, last night, he had called. A friend of his, whose car was not a heap of junk, was going to New York for the holidays and had offered to drop him off at Van Brunt. Heimrich had answered the telephone and had been greeted as "Dad." The days were long gone when he had been "sir" to young Michael Faye, who had been so grave and formal a child when Heimrich first met him and, a little later, became his stepfather.

Heimrich braked carefully at the stop sign before turning south on U.S. 9. The car felt as if it had thought of skidding but had changed its mind. Under the headlights the road looked merely wet. But under headlights a wet road and an icy road look much the same—too much the same. If it really iced, the traffic patrol cruisers would be having a rough time of it. And so would ambulance drivers. People didn't bother much with chains anymore. They relied on snow tires, which do not repay trust, even when they have metal studs set in them.

Heimrich drove slowly. He turned on the radio to the police channel. He cut in on a cruiser talking to traffic headquarters at

Troop K. "People sliding all over the goddamn roads," the trooper was reporting. The dispatcher said, "Yeah, there's a 'hazardous driving conditions' warning out."

"You'd think the damn fools would have sense enough to stay home," the cruiser responded.

Heimrich braked a little, carefully. The car did not skid. Ice heavier farther north, apparently. And he was going south. Sometimes a few miles make a lot of difference. Probably changed to snow by now at Washington Hollow, only a few miles behind him. As if answering his thought, a few flakes melted on the windshield. Better than freezing rain—at any rate for people who yearned for a white Christmas. That was not among Merton Heimrich's yearnings.

But there were no more snowflakes on the windshield and none swirled in the headlight beams. Instead, rain beat on the glass and on the Buick's roof. Getting warmer? Anyway, the car was. There wasn't much traffic. It seemed the trooper's damn fools were having sense enough to stay home. Slowly, the car continued south on U.S. 9, which is wide but no longer has three lanes, as it once had, with the disasters to be expected. A middle lane to use as a passing lane—for drivers going either way.

Heimrich pulled to the right and set his direction light blinking. He eased onto N.Y. 11-F and crept toward Cold Harbor. The shopping center just north of the village was busy; cars, confident of a right of way they did not have, pulled out of it. Heimrich pleaded no contest. One of the cars pulling out skidded as it turned, but came out of it and went on briskly. Of course, cars can skid on merely wet pavements, particularly on blacktops, which 11-F was. Making sure nobody was tailgating, Heimrich braked gently. The car swerved just perceptibly. Then the studs dug in. Yes, ice building now. He hoped Michael's friend knew how to drive on icy roads. Probably he did. Natives of Hanover, New Hampshire, or students at Dartmouth there either learned or quit driving. Michael would be graduated in the spring. Would he really, then, try his hand at being a tennis pro as, last summer, he had speculated that he might? Of course, playing in the number-one spot for Dartmouth, he had just beaten the number one of another Ivy League college in straight sets, the last at love. That might have given him ideas.

But, on another day of last summer, Michael had talked of law school and been thoughtful about Columbia. Maybe he could work his way through, or partly through. Maybe as a tennis instructor. Michael had no illusions about the income of policemen, even those with rank. Nor about the profits from *susan faye, fabrics,* on Van Brunt Avenue. Five miles or so on, N.Y. 11-F would, on passing "VAN BRUNT CITY LIMITS," became "VAN BRUNT AVENUE" and hold that title for a little over three miles. Only, of course, Van Brunt wasn't a city. It was not even a village. It was merely a gathering, in the town of Cold Harbor.

Heimrich passed VAN BRUNT CITY LIMITS, 35 MPH, and so entered Van Brunt. He was doing thirty. There was no doubt about the ice now. But the metal studs were doing their job. They had a heavier one coming, of course. Even on dry pavement, High Road presents some problems—twists and climbs its way into them.

Heimrich signaled for a right turn, although there were no following lights in the mirrors, and began to climb the narrow, twisting road toward the long, low house which had been a barn before it was the residence of Mrs. Michael Faye, née Upton, who had "married beneath her." In the old days, long before Heimrich had come to live in Van Brunt, or had even heard of it, almost everybody in Van Brunt had been "beneath" the Uptons. Oh, except the Jacksons and a few others, most notably, of course, the Van Brunts themselves.

The car skidded slightly on a steep curve. Heimrich recalled his mind from wandering and confined it to the task at hand, which was to get to the fire at home and to his wife, who probably had married beneath her for a second time. Uptons do not, habitually, marry policemen any more than they marry men with Irish names who come from the Flats.

The car skidded on another, even steeper, curve. Heimrich coaxed it back. The steel studs bit again. He ground up on High Road. He turned between two boulders into the driveway, which was even steeper than the road but had a gravel surface, which—so far, at any rate—gave better traction. Tomorrow, if this kept on, probably would be another story.

As he climbed the drive, the floodlight over the garage went on. Susan had been listening. She always listened. And the light had gone on, which was consoling. Heimrich drove into the garage, keeping well to the right. There would be room for Michael's friend's car, if it was a Volks. If it turned out to be a Cadillac, it would have to wait outside. Heimrich's Buick just grazed the wheelbarrow, which also lived in the garage.

When he came out into the breezeway between house and garage, the rain beat on him. The cement under his feet was glazed over. Cautiously, but still slithering a little, he reached for the wood stacked against the garage wall. It would be frozen together. It *was* frozen together. He should have put the tarp over it. He wrenched four logs loose and Susan opened the door for him. It was warming to have her so anticipate. Merton Heimrich could do with warming.

He carried the logs through the kitchen and piled them on the hearth. Flames were leaping in the fireplace. He had known they would be. He said "Hi" to Susan, who was wearing a red pantsuit, and she said, "Hi, darling." He started to reach toward her and remembered his wet raincoat and shed it. Then he reached for her. Eight years—a little more than eight years—they had been together. The years had not diminished the comfort, or the delight, they felt in each other's arms.

"I'll get them," Susan said. Heimrich sat in his chair in front of the fire and listened to the rattle of ice from the kitchen. Susan put the mixer on the table and sat beside him. He poured martinis into iced glasses, rubbed twisted lemon peel on the edges of the glasses, tossed the exhausted peels into the fire. They were just lifting their glasses to click them together when there was a splintering crash from somewhere outside. But the lights did not flicker. The glass jumped a little in Susan's hand. She steadied the hand and they clicked glasses. Then they sipped from the glasses and put them on the table, and Heimrich put his hand over the one of his wife's which had jumped with the sound of the falling tree. "He'll be all right," he told her. "Probably seem like nothing after New Hampshire. Anyway, they'll have the sand trucks out by now."

"Of course they'll be all right," Susan said. "I'm not worried. Not worried at all." She smiled at him what he knew to be a lie. And the hand which steadied the cigarette between her lips as he lighted it almost didn't tremble at all.

"But it's going to be a bad one, isn't it?" Susan said. "It's raining hard, isn't it? You can hear it on the roof."

There was no denying they could hear it on the roof. They could also hear it slashing against the windowpanes.

"Raining this hard, it usually warms up," Heimrich said. "Probably getting the wind shift. Gets around to the southwest and we'll be—"

Another tree crashed. The sound seemed closer. This time the lights flickered briefly. Then they steadied again.

"It's this damn waiting," Susan said. "You know it's going to happen and then it doesn't and then you just—go on waiting."

Mite, a black cat whose size belies his name, jumped to her lap and began to circle, adjusting it to his preference. He settled after only two turns. Susan put a hand on him and he began to purr. She said, "Where's Colonel, Mite?" A very large Great Dane stood up from behind the log cradle. He stood up slowly, as became his size and advancing years. One tries not to notice that pets lose sprightliness as they age. Heimrich said, "Good evening, Colonel," and the big dog moved to stretch in front of the fire. He thumped his tail twice on the floor. He was a dog of few words nowadays.

Susan and Merton Heimrich finished their drinks slowly. Between sips, Susan rested her glass on Mite's back, which happened to be uppermost. Each time she did so, Mite resumed his purr.

Heimrich looked at his watch. It was getting on toward seven. It had taken him almost twice as long as usual to get home from Washington Hollow.

"I'd planned a casserole," Susan said. "It'll take about an hour and then it will start to dry out. And the kids will be starving, of course."

"Naturally," Heimrich said and was looked at with a smile. He said, "Sorry, dear." (When they had first met, "naturally" had

amounted to a verbal tic in Heimrich's speech, even when he spoke
of events not at all natural. Susan had winced him out of the habit
—well, almost out of it.) He said, "When aren't they?"

"Never," Susan said. "And, more to the point, when are they
going to get here? And the casserole has to cook, not just warm up.
And we both know what's going to happen, sooner or later."

They both knew. Heimrich looked at the log cradle; at the
slightly steaming logs on the hearth. Better do something now.

"I could make us another round," Susan said. "You start to mix
drinks and people always come. Just when you're measuring. And
you forget whether you've already put the vermouth in."

She stood up, and another tree crashed down somewhere. The
somewhere sounded some distance away. Heimrich stood up, too.
Maybe the wind *has* shifted, he thought. Maybe the center has
gone north of us to badger Maine or Vermont. Or, of course, New
Hampshire. It will badger them with snow. And in the city, perhaps even as far up as Hawthorne Circle, it will be only rain.
We're caught in the middle, as usual.

He went to a window on the east side of the long room. Rain
was beating on it, which answered that. It was also beating on the
thermometer fixed to the window jamb. It was hard to read the column, with water streaming on it. The water was freezing on it.
Thirty. Maybe twenty-nine. Which answered *that*. The floodlight
above the garage was on—was still on. The power lines from the
road sagged under the heavy coating of ice. A young pine tree near
the drive was leaning down disconsolately, heavy with its burden.

Heimrich put his wet raincoat back on. He found a rain hat on
the upper shelf of the coat closet and put it on. He thought of
changing his shoes for heavier ones with ribbed soles. Instead, he
went to the kitchen and lifted a bag of Mite's cat litter. Enough in
it for Mite's immediate needs and also for his, Heimrich decided.

Susan was measuring gin into a mixing glass of ice. She looked
at him. "Wood," Heimrich said, and she nodded her head. He
opened the door to the breezeway, which was earning another
name—"galeway," at a guess. Wet wind poured into the kitchen.
Heimrich, edging out, scattered cat litter on the ice between door

and woodpile. Until it washed away, or froze in, it would provide a nonskid surface much superior to sand.

He wrenched logs apart. They were more tightly frozen together than they had been a little over half an hour before. One by one, and sometimes frozen together two by two, he skidded logs across the ice until they were near enough to be reached from the door. He skidded a dozen or so and thought that ought to last the night.

He inched his own way back. His foot slipped on the last step. Missed that part with the litter, he thought, and was close enough to grab the doorknob.

Susan helped him carry logs to the hearth, where at once they began to drip. Heimrich put one of the still-damp logs he had brought in earlier on the fire. The fire hissed its disapproval. Colonel got up, with condescending reluctance, and went back to where he had been before—in the warm airflow from the Heatolater vent which they had had installed the year before, a few weeks after the January ice storm.

They sat facing the fire again, and again clicked glasses. "To us," Susan said. "And to that wind shift of yours, darling."

The martinis were tart and cold. Susan had not forgotten the soupçon of vermouth.

"Only," she said, "it ought to be hot buttered rum on a night like this. Or mulled wine. Only, I never mulled any——"

She stopped. Merton heard it, too. It was loud enough to be heard over the angry wind.

A car with chains on it was clanking up the steep drive. One of the chains had a loose link banging against a fender.

They went to the kitchen door, Susan reaching it first. It was a Volks. Michael was driving it. His friend in the passenger seat was, only glimpsed through the driving rain, merely a blur—an unexpectedly small blur. Most of his friends were near his own six-foot height. "Standard tennis size," Susan had called them.

Michael drove the Volks into the garage; drove in slowly and carefully. Heimrich hoped he had left room enough. There was the power mower to consider. Michael was a careful boy. He would be considerate of the mower, and of his friend's Volks.

Merton reached around Susan, opened the door, and pulled her back against him, partly out of the driving rain. As the garage door began to open, he called "Watch the ice!" into the storm's roar.

They came out of the garage door, huddled figures in heavy short coats. Michael's friend was indeed small, stepping carefully on the ice, steadied by Michael's hands. Michael's friend wore a knitted cap, and hair streamed from it, lashed by the wind. Of course, boys wore their hair long these days.

Heimrich felt his wife stiffen just perceptibly in his arms and then his mind caught up with hers.

Michael's friend was not only small. Michael's friend was a girl.

Chapter 2

IN FRONT OF THE FIRE, with her heavy coat off, Michael's friend was most definitely a girl. The sweater she wore was loose; her slacks, of darker yellow than the sweater, did not cling to her slender legs. She did not, in costume, make a point of being a girl. She did not, Susan thought, need to.

"This is Joan Collins, Mother, Dad," Michael said, and stood beside the girl—stood close to her in front of the fire, but did not touch her. Although, Susan thought, he looks as if he wants to; as if, at any moment, he may put an arm around her. Susan said, "Good evening, Joan. Not that it is, obviously."

Joan Collins smiled at that. She had rather a wide smile on a somewhat thin face—an oddly decisive face. She's not over twenty, if that, Susan thought. But, she's a grown person, all the same. As she smiled, she shook her head slightly. Her long, straight brown hair flowed as she moved her head. What did Mother say when I was a little girl about somebody? "Her hair's so long she can sit on it." Something like that, in a tone of admiration. Hair had come full length again. She looked at her son, who was looking down at the girl beside him, and smiling that grave smile of his. His hair came only to the collar of his jacket. It was molded to his head. His sideburns reached only to his cheekbones. He didn't have a beard.

Which were silly things to be thinking of, under the circumstances.

"You kids probably could do with a drink," Merton said. (Or was he, a policeman sworn to uphold the law, offering to contribute to the delinquency of minors? Michael was—(come now; *remember*)—Michael was twenty. This accommodating friend of his? Well, eighteen, anyway. Both old enough to vote. So, old enough to be offered drinks.)

"I could do with one, Dad," Michael said. "It's been—well, rather a long drive. And not a very—comfortable one for the last few miles. Cold Harbor's blacked out, you know. We had the chains put on ten miles or so above Poughkeepsie. Had to wait in line. It's been a little bumpy since then. Not that it isn't a sweet little car, Joan's Beetle."

Joan had shaken her head to Heimrich's offer. Her long brown hair flowed again. It reached her waist.

"I'll just get warm," Joan said. Her voice was light; a little hurried.

She's a bit uneasy, Susan thought. Uncertain. As if—well, as if she had been brought here to meet parents. *The* parents.

"And get my hair dry." Joan reached back and touched her hair. "Which it almost is," she said. "Then I'll have to be getting on, I'm afraid. My father will be wondering. Starting to climb walls, probably. He's a little like that. So I'd better not have a drink, I guess. Since I'll be driving."

Michael did not seem to be listening. He was looking at Heimrich as if he were expecting something.

"No," Heimrich said. "On your way to New York, wouldn't it be? Not on this kind of a night."

"I was just going—" She hesitated. She looked up at Michael; then she looked at Susan.

"We know, dear," Susan said. "You were just going to drop Michael off on your way to the city to spend Christmas with your father. My son told us. Only, on this kind of a night—"

The lights went off. They made no fuss about it. They just quit being. The fire gave the only light in the room. It was a flickering light. Susan said, "Damn!"

"Anyway," Heimrich said, "the waiting's over." He put another log on the already leaping fire. "I'd better get the drinks made before the ice melts. And you'd better change your mind, Miss Collins. You won't be driving anywhere tonight. There's sherry, I think. If you'd rather."

"There *is* sherry," Susan said. "But—I'm afraid it's the kind you cook with."

It was the time some people said, "Whatever you're having." Susan found herself hoping Michael's girl wouldn't be among that some.

Joan looked up again at Michael. He smiled at her and nodded his head.

"Well," Joan Collins said, "maybe a little bourbon. But a very small one, please, Inspector." Her voice hesitated a trifle on "Inspector."

The poor child, Susan thought. Not only a parent. A police inspector.

"I'll get them, Dad," Michael said, and went toward the kitchen.

Mite came into sight. He had been lying more or less on top of Colonel, who was warm—warm enough even for a cat. Mite went over to Joan and smelled her shoes. Apparently they smelled all right, because he sat down in front of the fire and very close to it. A fire is even warmer than a dog.

Merton Heimrich went to the telephone. It might still be alive. Telephone wires are frequently, for some reason, more resolute than power lines in the face of adversity. Although they usually hitchhike up the same pole.

The telephone was alive. Heimrich dialed WE 6-1212. He listened. The seven o'clock temperature in New York City, which meant in Central Park, had been thirty-one. "Freezing rain, possibly becoming mixed with sleet and snow. Becoming all rain before ending early tomorrow, followed by slow clearing. Turning much colder Tuesday afternoon and night. Outlook for Christmas Day, mostly fair and seasonably cold."

When he turned from the telephone, Michael and Joan were sitting side by side in front of the fire. There were drinks on the table in front of them. Susan was on the other side of Michael. Joan Collins appeared to be sitting on her hair. She was listening to Michael.

"I know it doesn't happen much in Hanover," Michael was telling his mother. "In Hanover it rains, or it snows. And most of the time it stays below zero. And they know how to cope. Here—well, here it's different."

"I've noticed," Joan said.

Michael looked at her. Then he grinned at her. Even his wide smile had gravity in it, Heimrich thought. He hasn't changed much. He was a grave little boy.

"Here it's in between," Michael said. "Once every year or so, we get—well, what we're getting now. And the power goes off. Sometimes for—how long, Dad?" He turned in his chair so that he faced his tall, somewhat massive stepfather.

"Six days is the longest I remember, son," Heimrich said. "You were about ten then."

"He was eleven," Susan said. "And it was seven days, as I remember it. It was something of a drag."

"We didn't have any lights," Michael said, "or anything to cook with, except Dad roasted potatoes in the ashes. It was—oh, I guess, exciting. For a kid, I mean. Only, there wasn't any water. Hardly any. Isn't that right, Mother?"

"We had to be very careful with it," Susan said. "We get our water from a deep well, Joan." ("Joan" or "Miss Collins"? Joan, it seemed.) "An electric pump, of course. And no way of telling how much is in the pressure tank."

"And no heat," Heimrich said. "Because you can't light an oil furnace with a match."

"Damn it," Susan said. "That casserole." She looked at Merton and her eyebrows went up.

"Yes," Heimrich said. "I'd think so, dear. If its generator went on. And, Miss Collins, it's freezing up in New York, too. And not expected to stop before morning."

"They're talking about the inn, Joan," Michael said. "They leave things out sometimes. The inn—the Old Stone Inn, it's called —has its own generator. It goes on when the power stops."

Heimrich's second martini—what remained of it—was still on the table in front of the fire. It would have warmed up there. Still. Heimrich crossed the room and reached down between the two and retrieved his drink. It was just as warm as he had feared.

"*Darling,*" Susan said. "It must be a—a hot buttered martini by now. I'll fix——"

But she stopped, because he shook his head at her. Also, he had emptied his glass. He went back across the room to the telephone. It was still alive. He dialed. He waited.

He said "Mary?" to Mary Cushing, who managed the inn for whoever owned it now. The ownership of country inns changes from time to time. He said, "This is Heimrich, Mary," and listened for a moment. He said, "It certainly is. Lousy is the word for it. It went on all right?" He listened. He said, "Four in half an hour or so?" He listened again and said, "Fine, we'll be along. And, Mary, two rooms for overnight?" He waited, but only for a moment. "No," he said. "Have to keep the fires going. For young Michael and a friend of his. Yes, two rooms. The way they want it." He said, thanks and, again, that they'd be along.

He went back to the fire and stood in front of it. He intervened between Mite and Mite's fire. Mite was reasonably courteous about it, although he did speak, briefly. He moved enough so that the heat hit him full on.

"All set," Heimrich said. "It's a lousy night. The generator went on and, Mary says, they're lighted up like a Christmas tree. Food for four, lodging for two."

Joan Collins said, "Two, Inspector?"

"You two," Heimrich said. "Susan and I'll have to keep—" He checked himself before he said "the home fires burning." He said, "Keep a fire going so we don't freeze up."

"We don't really—" Joan said, and stopped abruptly, and looked at Michael. His expression didn't say anything. But then he smiled rather briefly.

"Need two rooms," Susan finished, but only in her mind. She was not surprised. She had supposed as much from the way the two looked at each other; the way they carefully did not touch each other. She probably thinks we're very rigid, Susan thought; very old and—and proper? Too old to understand? They're—they're so very young. And think we're so very old.

"So," Heimrich said, and poked the fire back. He looked at it for a moment, and decided he could risk another log. He pulled the screen meshes together across the fireplace and stood the heavy fire-tool rack in front of them.

Mite was not pleased by this. He said so. He moved back to the warmth of the Heatolater vent. After a moment, Colonel sighed deeply and went to join him. A dog just gets settled and he has to move again.

"So," Heimrich said, "we'll just use one car, I think. Leave yours here until tomorrow, Miss Collins."

Michael and Joan stood up, Joan a little hesitantly. She said, "Only, Mrs. Heimrich—my things."

"They'll be quite safe in the——" Heimrich said, but Susan, gently, broke in on that.

"She means her night things, dear," Susan said, in the compassionate tone women use for the obtusity of males. "We'll put whatever you need in the big car, Joan. Your overnight things."

"But," Joan said, "I can't go to a restaurant looking like this. Dressed like this."

"On a night like this," Susan told her, "everybody will be wearing whatever they happened to have on when the lights went off. Anything warm enough, anyway. But we'll take you whatever you want, my dear."

They went out through the kitchen, which was closest to the garage door. They went cautiously across the breezeway ice. Michael put an arm around the slim girl to steady her. (Also, Susan thought, because there was a reason to hold her close.) Heimrich put an arm about his wife's shoulders. (Yes, Susan thought, for the same reasons. But the kids won't notice that, or believe that possible.)

What Joan needed was one of the two largish suitcases which occupied the back seat of the Volks and a small overnight case which Michael extracted from the little trunk which occupied the space allotted the engine in other cars. They fitted handily in the Buick's trunk. The Buick made rather a fuss about starting, and

Heimrich swore at it. Perhaps, sometime, Detroit would be able to combine antipollution devices with an engine willing to run. Heimrich rather doubted it.

Finally, the engine seemed content. It stalled, of course, when Heimrich put the pointer at "R." But it agreed to start up again.

They inched down High Road. They stopped at The Corners, where the traffic lights were not working. There was no traffic on Van Brunt Avenue. But the avenue had been sanded; 11-F was, after all, a state road. It rated at least a modicum of sand.

Even with the studded tires, the Buick tried to skid as it was turned into the brightly lighted parking lot of the Old Stone Inn. Heimrich curbed it. There were a dozen or so cars in the lot. They seemed to cringe in the damp cold. Four of them were already iced over. The others were obviously only recently expelled from the dry refuges of nearby garages. Rural areas are suspended precariously at the ends of overhead wires. Within a ten-mile radius, only the inn had light and heat. A few houses, of course, had bottled gas to cook with. During ice storms, the less provident Van Brunt residents turned to the inn, if they were within creeping distance.

The way from car to taproom entrance had been sanded. The footing was tricky but not really difficult. But Michael held his girl close in a protecting arm as they walked the few yards to the door. So. Heimrich did as much for Susan.

The taproom was bright and warm and a fire leaped in a fireplace. There were a dozen or so people at tables, tables nearest the fire being favored. Susan and Merton knew all but two—the two who, alone, wore "party" clothes—the man a dinner jacket, the woman a long dress. The rest wore what the blackout had caught them in, which was largely sweaters and slacks. Oliver Finley also wore climbing boots. The Finleys did live at the top of a considerable rise above the Hudson.

They found a table, not as close to the fire as they would have liked. All right. First come, first warmed.

"We can eat here," Susan told Joan. "Or in the main dining room. There isn't any fire in there, but the food comes quicker. On the other hand, the drinks come slower. We take our choice."

It was a way of welcoming Michael's girl in. The welcome was accepted. Joan Collins smiled, more warmly than she had before. She said, "Here's nice, isn't it? Only, I'd like——"

Michael did not let her finish. He stood up, although he had not really sat down.

"I'll get your things," Michael said. "Dad?"

Heimrich tossed him the car keys. Michael went out into the rain.

The bar waitress came. In deference to the weather outside, if in defiance of the temperature in the taproom, she wore a sweater over her uniform. She said, "Good evening, Inspector, Mrs. Heimrich, isn't it a terrible night?" All over Van Brunt, the town of Cold Harbor, a considerable part of the Northeastern seaboard, people would be telling other people what a terrible night it was.

"Awful," Heimrich said. "Two very dry martinis, up, no olive. Tell him twists, but not dropped in. Two bourbons on the rocks. A little extra water in one." He looked at Joan Collins, who smiled and nodded agreement. "And we'll eat in here. Order later."

"We're being sort of busy tonight," the waitress said. "People not being able to cook at home and all. Because of this awful weather. Two martinis up and hold the olives. Two bourbons on the rocks. Old Forrester be all right, Inspector? Because that's what Joe's serving tonight, it being so close to Christmas."

Not really a non sequitur, Heimrich thought, and he said Old Forrester would be fine. The waitress said, "Right away, Inspector," and went toward the bar. Cold, wet air flowed briefly into the room, blowing Michael in front of it. Michael kicked the door closed, but it didn't stay closed. He had to put down the larger of the cases he was carrying and make the door secure. He carried the cases to the table but did not put them down.

"May as well see about the rooms while I'm about it," he said. "Want to come along, Joanie?"

Joan looked at Susan, who said, "Of course, dear. You'll want to freshen up after that long drive." The Heimrichs watched the two go across the taproom and under the arch into the small lobby of the Old Stone Inn.

"Well," Merton Heimrich said.

Susan said she couldn't agree more.

"Been a bit of a problem if it hadn't been for the storm," Merton said. "With only Michael's room for a guest room and the only bed in it a double."

"Problem for us, dear," Susan said. "Not for them, I think, don't you?"

Heimrich said, "Mmm."

"You've only to watch them," Susan told him.

He said "Mmm" again. Then he said, "I thought mothers were supposed to feel upset about it. All—I don't know. Bothered. A feeling of desertion."

Susan said, "Did you, dear?" She looked at him.

"No, I guess not," Heimrich said. "Not you, Susan." He paused and looked at her across the table. "No," he said. "Not you." He offered her a cigarette and lighted it for her and lighted one of his own.

"Of course," he said, "if it hadn't been for the storm, she'd have dropped him and driven on to New York. That was the plan, wasn't it?"

"What Michael told me, dear. But of course, he just said a 'friend.' She seems a very nice girl, don't you think? A little ill at ease, maybe, but under the circumstances——"

"If the power hadn't gone off," Heimrich said, "and she'd have decided to stay over—it would have raised a problem? For us. Perhaps for them, too."

"The proprieties, you mean? We're not much for the proprieties, are we? Is Dartmouth coeducational, do you know? Because I've always thought of it as—well, rather rugged. Football, and that sort of thing."

"I believe it is, nowadays," Heimrich told her. "Coed, I mean. The climate's rugged enough, from what Michael's told us. It's Ivy, of course. All Ivy seems to be going coed. I wonder if——"

"Here we are, Inspector," the bar waitress said. "The martinis for you two, is that right?"

Heimrich told her that that was right.

"And the others?"

The others would be right along, he told her. She could put their drinks down. And, as long as she had brought them, she could leave the menus. She left the drinks and the menus. She obeyed a beckoning finger from another table.

Michael came through the passage into the taproom. He said, "All set. Very nice rooms over the parking lot. Did I say how good it is to see you both?"

"I don't remember you did," Susan said, and smiled at her son. "We took it for granted. She seems like a very nice girl, Michael. She's going to Dartmouth, too?"

"Sophomore," Michael said. "And her father's an English professor. Her stepfather, that is. Professor Faneworth. Her real father is named Collins—James Collins, I think it is. She spends the Christmas holidays with him. Court order, or something. Yes, Mother, Joan's quite a girl." He looked over his shoulder toward the archway.

"She said she'd be right along," he said. "I hope she—well, doesn't get lost, or anything."

"She's a girl, son," Heimrich said. "Probably wants to change her clothes. It takes girls longer, Michael." He paused. "Anyway," he said, "welcome home."

The three of them clicked glasses. But Michael put his down without drinking from it. He looked again toward the archway.

Joan Collins was not coming through it. A tall, lean man—lean in spite of a bulky, fleece-lined coat—was coming into the taproom. He looked at the Heimrichs and raised a hand to his bare head in salute.

Heimrich said, "Hi, Sam."

The lean man came to their table and looked down at them, smiling. He said, "Hi, Susan dear. Hi, M.L. Hello, Michael. Thought you weren't going to be able to make it."

Michael said, "Good evening, Mr. Jackson. I got a ride down at the last minute."

"Just the three of you?" Sam Jackson said, and looked briefly at the empty chair.

Susan shook her head.

"Michael's friend who brought him down's going to join us," she said. "But have a drink with us, Sam. You're stuck in the village?"

"Staying overnight in the office," Jackson said. "No use skidding up and down hills in this kind of weather. Also, got some odds and ends to go over."

The office of Samuel Jackson, attorney-at-law, was across Van Brunt Avenue from the inn. The house he lived alone in was up even steeper grades from Van Brunt Center than the Heimrichs'.

"Also, Friday's decided he's got lumbago." Jackson's "man Friday" was named Friday, which was a coincidence which his friends in Van Brunt no longer made much of. "Well—" He reached toward the vacant chair. But he stopped reaching when Joan Collins came out of the lobby and into the taproom, and headed toward the table. Joan had changed to a gray woolen dress, which did a good deal for her figure. She had also, Susan noticed, redone her face.

My son has good judgment, Susan thought. She said, "This is Samuel Jackson, Joan. An old friend of ours. Miss Collins, Sam. She drove Michael down from Hanover."

Jackson pulled the chair out for the girl and said, "Miss Collins." Joan sat on it, and said, "Mr. Jackson." Then she said, "We didn't pick a very good day for it, did we?"

"Icebound," Jackson said. "But you made it. Hanover must be even worse. Spent six weeks there during the war. Naval indoctrination. Teaching youngish officers not to salute CPOs. Got down to fifty below one morning when we were forming up to march to breakfast. Breath froze on our bridge coats."

"It gets cold, all right," Joan said. "I live there, Mr. Jackson."

"Probably nice in the summer," Jackson said. "Well—" He added, "Pleasant to meet you, Miss Collins," and went to a table on the other side of the room. The bar waitress carried a drink to the table, not waiting for it to be ordered.

"Sam looks tired," Susan said.

Heimrich agreed. "Also," he said, "Sam's getting along."

They drank, Joan Collins very slowly, somewhat tentatively. The others had finished before she had drunk more than half her watered whiskey. After a few moments, during which Joan took an evidently experimental sip from her glass, Heimrich raised a hand for the waitress. They studied menus; they ordered. When the waitress had written on her order pad, Heimrich looked at Susan, who nodded her head. "And two martinis." He looked at Joan, who shook her head. Heimrich said, "Michael?" Michael Faye shook his head.

"I really mean rare on my steak," Heimrich told the waitress, who said, "I know, Inspector," and went away.

Merton and Susan did not hurry with their drinks. They had each a sip left when a busboy brought a heavy tray in, and lowered it, a little precariously, Susan thought, to a service table. He was a local boy. One of the Purvis boys, Heimrich thought. Jacob? Perhaps Jeremiah, Junior?

They ate. Heimrich's steak was medium rare. Susan's was medium. Both Michael and Joan ordered roast lamb. It wasn't pink, but they hadn't specified pink. Probably, Heimrich thought, wouldn't have got it if they had. The cuisine of the Old Stone Inn is Middle America. No "raw" meat.

Chapter 3

The weather had not improved. If anything, it had worsened. The rain still fell in sheets; it still froze where it hit. Ice thickened on the roads; trees knelt under their burdens of ice. Even with the Buick's windows closed, they could hear trees crashing down. The defroster kept the windshield clear of ice. On the rear window, ice formed; the rearview mirror disclosed only the vaguest of blurs. The Buick floundered on the steep curves of High Road. The studs bit in enough—just barely enough. When Heimrich turned from the road into the drive, the car skidded, not quite into one of the boulders.

It was no night to be out. Most of those who had come to the Old Stone Inn to huddle from the storm were still huddled there when Heimrich said, "Well?" to Susan, and added, "You can still change your mind. Mary can fix you up."

"No," Susan said, and stood up. "Whither thou goest."

Merton Heimrich had not had much hope. He had been listened to, tolerantly. When he pointed out that he, by himself, could keep the fire going so the house wouldn't freeze up, Susan had said, "Of course, dear." When he had said it would be smelly in the house with the oil stove going in the kitchen and that she hated the smell even more than he did, she had said that she'd try to stay out of the kitchen. And when he had given her a last chance, she had stood up from the table and begun to put her storm coat on.

"I'll pick you up in the morning," Heimrich had told Michael and his pretty friend. "Supposed to clear up tomorrow. Sun will thaw the roads."

"Except where evergreens shade them," Michael had said to that.

Neither of them mentioned that sunshine wouldn't bring the power back; that only men could do that, and it wouldn't be by tomorrow.

They signaled good night to Sam Jackson, finishing his coffee at his small table by the wall. Sam was lucky—only a couple of hundred yards to walk across Van Brunt Avenue.

"And he's had sense enough to hold onto a couple of Aladdin lamps, he told me once," Heimrich said, as they got into the Buick.

And now, a moderately perilous few miles accomplished, they were ready to get out of it. There was room to open the car door partway, beside Joan's still ice-sheathed Volks. They squeezed out. Mite's cat litter was frozen over in the breezeway, but the cement was still faintly gritty underfoot. And the lock of the kitchen door still hadn't frozen—not completely, anyway.

The fire had burned down, but no logs had rolled out of it. Colonel and Mite were lying in front of the fire, Mite protectively encircled by Colonel's right foreleg. Mite is Colonel's cat; has been Colonel's cat since, when he was a mite of a kitten, Colonel found him and brought him home in his mouth. Deposited on sunny flagstones of the terrace, Mite had been a very wet small cat. He had also been a very indignant one.

Heimrich put more logs on the fire, somewhat impeded by the livestock. He lugged the emergency oil heater in from the garage and lighted it in the kitchen. It began to stink, as always.

Susan found candles and lighted them. It wasn't really cold in the house. Not if you stayed close to the fire. She set water trickling from faucets in both bathrooms. The oil heater would keep water from freezing in the kitchen pipes. Anyway, it always had before.

Between them, they hauled the mattress from Michael's double bed and stretched it in front of the fire. Mite got to it first, and curled himself in the middle. They had nightcaps in front of the fire before they dislodged Mite and, fully dressed except for their storm coats, lay down on the mattress.

Heimrich put an arm around his wife. She was shivering a little, but the shivering lessened as he held her closer. Of course, it was a cold, dank night. And the car heater hadn't really got going on the trip from the inn to the house above the Hudson. And, probably, it had been an evening trying on her nerves. Not that Joan Collins didn't seem to be a nice girl, in addition to being a very pretty one.

When she had stopped shivering, Susan went to sleep. Merton Heimrich was not so lucky. He lay very still beside his wife, quiet so as not to waken her. He kept his arm around her, realizing that it probably would go to sleep before the rest of him did. He listened to the slash of rain against windows and to the rush of the wind. Now and then he heard, distantly, the crashing fall of still another tree. Some of the trees would merely lose boughs. It would be a bad night for ancient apple trees—particularly for them. Old apple trees are brittle. And, doggedly, sometimes a little wistfully, they go on producing apples. An example to—to what? Heimrich couldn't quite remember.

The fire was burning all right. It would be an hour, maybe, before he had to put another log on. It was hot in front of the fire. Hot enough to singe Susan's pantsuit? He didn't think—

He didn't think at all. He slept.

The alarm clock wakened him. It couldn't be morning yet. He couldn't have slept that long. It was still dark. Of course, it stayed dark late just before Christmas. The alarm clock kept on ringing.

It took Heimrich only thirty seconds or so to remember that they didn't have an alarm clock. Susan stirred in the circle of his arm. She said, "Who at this hour?" her voice muffled by sleep. And then, "Don't answer the damn—" and did not finish, but went back to sleep instead.

Heimrich switched on the flashlight he had taken to bed with him and went to answer the telephone. He was wide awake by the time he answered it. So was Susan. Heimrich spoke his name into the telephone.

"Dad?" Michael's word was hurried; the pitch of his voice high.

Heimrich said, "Yes, Michael?"

"Dad, a man's been killed. Here at the inn. In the parking lot. And, Dad, it was Mr. *Jackson.* And Joan thinks somebody meant to kill him. Dad, Joan saw it happen. From the window of her room. She says whoever it was couldn't have helped seeing him, because the lot was all lighted up. And——"

"*Sam* Jackson," Heimrich said. "You're sure he's dead?"

"Dad," Michael said, "They brought him into the inn. The bartender and that Purvis kid. He—well, the car ran over his head. It must've been one of the wheels with chains on it. It's awful to look at, Dad. And Joanie saw it happen. *Saw* it. Mrs. Cushing's phoned for an ambulance. But—well, an ambulance won't do any good. If it ever gets here. And——"

"Listen, Michael. Ask Mrs. Cushing to ring the substation in Cold Harbor. Ask whoever's on there to call the barracks and have them try to get hold of Forniss. Tell him to try to get down. I'll be down myself. Get Miss Collins to have a drink, son. And have one yourself."

"I already got her one, Dad. She's up by the fire with it. She's—well, she's pretty shaky. Terribly shaky, actually. Mrs. Cushing's doing what she can, but——"

"Try to help Mrs. Cushing, son. I'll be along. Right?"

"Yes, Dad. She—she just keeps crying. And sort of shaking all over. I'm afraid——"

"Yes, Michael. She's had quite a shock. Try to calm her down. I'll be along."

He put the receiver back in its cradle.

Susan wasn't asleep anymore. She was sitting up on the matress, hugging her knees. She was staring at him. She said, "Something's happened to Sam? That's it, isn't it? To *Sam!*"

"Yes," Heimrich said. "Sam's been killed, dear. A car hit him in the parking lot. Michael's girl saw it happen, Michael says. And thinks the driver meant to hit him. The boy's very excited. Words sort of tumble out of him. I'll have——"

"Yes," Susan said. "I know. Wouldn't it be better if I—?"

"No, Susan," Heimrich said. "No use both of us. Keep the fire going, and watch that damn stove. Flares up sometimes. And try to get some sleep. All right?"

"It'll have to be, I guess," Susan Heimrich said. "Be careful, dear. Hadn't you better put the chains on?"

Heimrich had got heavy boots out of the hall closet—boots with ridged soles. He was lacing them up. He said, "Mmm." Which meant, Susan knew, that he wasn't going to put the chains on, because putting on tire chains takes time and is also a grubby, mildly hazardous job.

When Heimrich finished with his boots and stood up, Susan, too, stood, and went to him. She held his storm coat, which was wet on the outside. She put a hand on each of his arms, and pressed them. She said, "Be careful, darling. It's an awful night."

He said, "Yes, dear, I'll be careful," and kissed her.

She went with him to the kitchen door. She held the flashlight, its guiding beam on the glazed cement of the breezeway.

It wasn't, Heimrich thought, raining quite as hard. And he thought the wind was shifting a little, from northeast to, it was to be hoped, northwest. Which would, in some hours, make a difference. Not, of course, while he was driving on ice to Van Brunt Center and the Old Stone Inn. Or while Lieutenant Charles Forniss was driving the much longer, and equally iced, way from the barracks of Troop K, New York State Police. If, of course, they had managed to get hold of Forniss.

He backed the Buick out of the garage. For once, it didn't stall. He headed it down the steep drive. It tried to skid, and he wouldn't let it. He went down High Road at about ten miles an hour. The sand which had been spread on Van Brunt Avenue helped a little—made fifteen miles an hour reasonably safe.

The inn's parking lot was a sheet of ice, but at least it was lighted ice. There were still cars in it. Heimrich parked as close as he could to the taproom entrance. As he got out he saw a blurred

red stain nearer the center of the lot. Blood, probably; frozen blood, by now. Sam Jackson's blood.

It was only about ten thirty when Heimrich went into the taproom. It had been a few minutes before nine when he and Susan had gone out of it, and flicked good-bye to Sam Jackson, who was having a brandy with his coffee at a table against the wall, and who had seemed abstracted when he gave his familiar loose-armed salute to them.

There were still people in the taproom now, and the fire was still blazing. Most of the people were locals; most of them Heimrich knew. They were lingering over coffee and, in most cases, drinks. It was a night to linger, to postpone. Sometime, they would have to leave light and warmth and venture into an inhospitable night of ice. But not yet. Have another cup of coffee; another sip from a glass. Things were not going to get any better, but things could be put off.

Michael got up from a table near the door. He was alone at the table; he drained a cup of coffee as he stood. There was no sign of Joan Collins.

"The ambulance hasn't come, Dad," Michael said. The words still seemed to tumble from his mouth—the mouth from which words usually came so distinctly and so gravely. "He—the body's—in the lobby. They've covered it with something. I suppose—suppose you'll want to look. It's pretty awful, Dad."

Heimrich has seen many things which were pretty awful to see. He couldn't remember the first time. He could remember how it had felt, how it had sickened and unnerved. He could feel, again, what young Michael was feeling now.

He said, "Joan, Michael?"

"Up in her room," Michael said. "Mrs. Cushing's with her. She —I'm afraid she's terribly shaken up, Dad. She just cries and shakes her head. And sort of trembles."

"Naturally," Heimrich said. "I'll have to talk to her, son. Have her tell me what she saw. Did Mrs. Cushing get in touch with the substation? With Charlie Forniss?"

"The Lieutenant's off duty, they told her. They're trying to find him. A trooper's on his way down from Cold Harbor, I think."

"Yes," Heimrich said. "We'd better go up and see Miss Collins." He started toward the lobby and Michael went with him. But then Heimrich stopped and turned back to face the dozen people in the room. All of them were loroking at him.

"I'm Inspector Heimrich of the state police," he said. Not that all but two—the two who by their dress, were up from the city—didn't know he was Inspector Heimrich of the state police, known to most of them as "M.L." "There's been an accident, and we have to look into it. I'd appreciate it if all of you would stay around for a while. Shouldn't be too long. O.K.?"

Nobody said it wasn't O.K. Larry Newcombe, of Laurence Newcombe Associates, Realtors, said, "Sure, M.L."

Heimrich and Michael Faye went out of the taproom and into the small lobby. There was nobody in the lobby. Nobody living. The body of Samuel Jackson was on a narrow sofa along one wall. A damn uncomfortable sofa, as Heimrich remembered it. That wouldn't be bothering Sam Jackson now. The sofa was barely long enough for his body, which was covered with a sheet.

Heimrich lifted one end of the sheet and looked at the face of a longtime friend—at what was left of the face. It was, as Michael had said, pretty awful. The wheel which had gone over Jackson's head had indeed had tire chains on it.

Michael did not look. He stood at the foot of a wide staircase and looked up it, and waited. Heimrich put the sheet back and joined his son—oh, stepson, to be sure, but it didn't feel like that. They went up the stairs together, and down a corridor.

There were two closed doors at the end of the corridor. Michael knocked on one of them and somebody on the other side of the room said, "Yes?"

"Michael. And Dad's with me, Mrs. Cushing." He turned the knob and opened the door.

The room was large. There was a heavy, darkwood double bed against one wall. At the end of the room there were two wide, double-hung windows, with curtains drawn partly over them. In one wall there was a fireplace, with logs burning in it—burning down a little. Joan Collins was sitting in one of two chairs in front of the fire and Mary Cushing was sitting beside her in the other. Joan wore a quilted white robe. Within Joan's reach there was a round table with a lamp on it and, beside the lamp, a small brandy glass. The little glass was, Heimrich thought, almost full.

Michael went across the room and crouched beside Joan. He took both of her hands in his and she put her head down on his shoulder. Her long hair flowed over his shoulder.

Heimrich went down the room to the windows and parted the curtains over one of them. He looked out on the lighted parking lot, almost directly down on his own ice-glazed Buick. The ice on the pavement partly obscured the painted lines which marked parking slots.

Rain was not slashing these windows on the south side of the inn. He could, however, see driving rain in the light from the floods, one fixed to the roof of the inn and the other on a pole across from it. Very bright and welcoming, the Old Stone Inn kept its parking lot.

Heimrich turned back to the room. In the wall opposite the fire there was a door. The door was closed. A connecting door between this bedroom and the next, almost certainly. And the next room Michael's? Probably.

He went to the three in front of the fire. Mary Cushing got up and motioned. Heimrich nodded his head and smiled at her and took the chair beside Joan Collins. After a moment, she lifted her head and looked at him. She wasn't crying at the moment. She had been.

"He's dead, isn't he? The man I saw. He'd have to be dead, wouldn't he?" Her voice was almost steady.

"Yes, Joan," Heimrich said, "he's dead. It was Sam Jackson—the man we introduced to you at dinner."

"I'm sorry," the girl said. "I'm terribly sorry."

"We all are, Joan. Feel up to telling me what you saw? If you don't—well, it can wait awhile, I suppose."

"I don't think it will get any easier if I put it off," the girl said. She turned in her chair to face the big man beside her. Michael let go her hands. He did so very slowly. The release was almost a caress.

"It was this way," Joan said. "I came up early. Right after you and Mrs. Heimrich left. I was tired and—relaxed, I guess you'd call it. From being in where it was warm. And dry, of course. After that awful rain. Is it still raining, Inspector?"

"Yes," Heimrich said. "It's still raining. Not quite so hard, maybe. Michael didn't come up here with you?"

"I asked him not to," she said. "I—I just wanted to go to sleep. And call Father first to tell him I wouldn't get there tonight, and that I was all right. Before he started climbing walls. I told you he was like that, didn't I?"

"Yes, Joan. You said something about it. You called your father in New York and reassured him. Then?"

"There was a fire burning. I sat in front of it—right here—for a few minutes. Then I went to bed. I went to sleep right away, I think. Then—"

She had, she thought, slept only a short time. Not more than half an hour, probably. She wakened because she got too hot. "With the heavy blankets over me." And there had not seemed to be any air in the room.

She remembered, then, that she had forgotten to open a window before she went to bed. "I can't ever sleep unless there's air coming in." She had parted the curtains at one of the windows, and pulled one sash up a little. She had thought cold, wet air would come rushing in. It did not. She raised the sash higher and, as she did so, looked out on the lighted parking lot.

"A man came out. A tall man, wearing a heavy, short coat. He came out from the inn, I thought through the door from the barroom—the place where we all had dinner. He started to walk across the lot. Toward the street, I thought. He didn't seem to be afraid to walk on the ice."

Sam Jackson had been wearing heavy shoes, with ribbed soles such as Heimrich was now wearing, when he walked to his death. Walked confidently, it appeared. Heimrich waited. Joan had stopped speaking. She was no longer looking at Merton Heimrich. She was looking into the fire. When she spoke again, she seemed to be telling her story to the fire.

"When he was about a third of the way across the lot, this car backed into him. Backed very suddenly. Its engine must have been running. It was as if—as if it had been waiting for him. Had known he was coming and been waiting. It hit him and knocked him down. I don't think it ran over him. Not then. He seemed to be trying to get up."

The car—a big car—had backed around, and then gone forward. "It sort of jumped forward." The big car had struck the tall man again. "This time it ran over him. Over—over his head, it looked like. And—just went on going. It had chains on, didn't it? I heard them clanking."

"Yes," Heimrich said, "the car had chains on. Could you tell what kind of car it was, Joan?"

"It was a big car, I think. A big station wagon, it looked like. That's what it was, I think. A big station wagon. *And it didn't have its lights on, Inspector.* I think it turned them on just as it started to go out into the street. And then—well, then I began to knock on Michael's door. Pounded on it, I guess. And to call to him. The door between my room and his, Inspector."

"I assumed Michael's friend would be another boy," Mary Cushing said, from a chair at the desk counter across the room. "You didn't say, you know, when you called up about the rooms. If I'd known——"

"It's all right, Mary," Heimrich said. "No harm done. Made it easier for Miss Collins, actually. Michael had come up by then? Was in his room when you knocked on the door?"

"I was there, Dad," Michael said. "I'd just come up. Joanie was —well, in a sort of panic."

"With plenty of reason," Heimrich said. "Notice what color this station wagon was, Joan?"

"No, I'm afraid not. Dark-colored, I think. But it—it all happened so fast. It was so—unbelievable. It was—well, sort of all over before I realized it was happening at all."

"Things do happen like that," Heimrich told her. "And, of course, with its lights off, you had no chance to see the license number?"

"I wouldn't have thought to look anyway," Joan said. "I can't pretend I would have. I'm not a very good witness, am I?"

"Good enough, Joan. Better than most, matter of fact. The car stopped, I suppose. Before it went into the highway. After it turned on its lights. Did you see which way it turned? I mean, up or down. That would be north or south."

"I'm afraid I didn't watch, Inspector. I—I was trying to get to Michael. To tell him what I'd seen happen."

"Yes," Heimrich said. "Was there more than one person in this car, could you tell?"

She couldn't. It had been dark in the car.

"But it was your impression, your feeling, that whoever was driving backed into Sam Jackson deliberately? And then deliberately ran over him?"

"There's a lot of light in the parking lot," Joan said. "Even with all the rain, it was bright enough. I don't see how anybody could have missed seeing him. He was so tall. So—visible."

"Yes," Heimrich said. "Sam Jackson was a tall man. Can you show me where this wagon was parked?"

Michael helped the girl up from the chair. She didn't appear to need help. She was obviously not averse to a consoling touch. Michael went with them to the window.

"About there, I think," Joan said. She pointed to a place about halfway between the taproom door and the street. "It was nosed up to the logs." Logs formed a barrier between lot and what, in summer, was a flower bed. "It was all by itself. The other cars were parked nearer the door."

"Nothing on either side of it," Heimrich said. "And you think the motor was running?"

"It must have been. It backed up so fast. And I didn't hear the starter going. And—wait a minute. I remember now. Fumes were coming out of the exhaust pipe. I could see them."

"Yes," said Heimrich. "A wet, cold night like this, the exhaust would show up. One exhaust pipe or two, did you notice?"

"I'm not sure, Inspector. If I had to guess, it would be two. It—it all happened so fast."

"You saw a lot, Joan," Heimrich said. "You're a very good witness. I suppose you haven't any sleeping pills with you?"

"Sleeping pills?" She spoke as of something obviously alien, unheard of. "I never have any trouble going to sleep."

Heimrich looked at Michael, who shook his head. He looked at Mary Cushing.

"No, M.L. But I can have some warm milk sent up. Warm milk and aspirin."

"That'll be fine," Heimrich said. "You get some sleep now, Joan. You too, son. I'll pick you up in the morning. Though it probably will be later on before the roads are safe. Even if it stops raining and the sun comes out."

"A train?"

"There's a seven forty-eight. But that's pretty early. And with the power off, it may not be running. We'll see in the morning. All right?"

She nodded her head.

"So," Heimrich said, "drink the milk Mrs. Cushing will send up to you and take the aspirins. And Michael will be right next door. And I wouldn't lock the door, son. So Joan can get you if she needs you. Not that she will, of course."

"We hadn't planned to lock—" He broke off.

Heimrich did not appear to hear him. He said, "Sleep well, both of you," and went out of the room and down the stairs.

The body of Sam Jackson still lay on the narrow, hard sofa in the lobby. Heimrich was not surprised. The Cold Harbor hospital has only two ambulances. On a night like this, with driving conditions what they were, the ambulances would have more pressing duties than the removal of corpses. The dead are dead; the living may yet be kept so.

The brightness in the taproom reminded Heimrich of a question he had forgotten to ask, and should have asked. When she went to open her bedroom window, had she turned on the lights? Or found her way by the flickering light of the fire? He paused before he went on into the taproom. Should he go back up and ask?

If I had been waiting in a car for a man to back into, to run over outside an inn, I'd have looked up for a lighted window, Heimrich thought. For somebody who might be watching; for the silhouette of that person. Such a check would be only prudent. Maybe I'd better go back and find out.

He decided not to. His reappearance, his question, would further frighten an already tense young woman, a girl who already probably would be tormented by ugly dreams. Michael was a strong and remarkably quick young man. He would be in the next room and the door between the rooms would not be locked.

Probably won't even be closed, Heimrich thought, and went on into the taproom.

Chapter 4

WHEN HE WENT into the taproom, everybody in it looked at him. Expectantly? Heimrich thought so. At a glance, he thought that all who had been asked to wait had waited. No. The couple dressed for a party were no longer at their table. Joe Shepley, the barman, was still behind the bar. He stood up when Heimrich went over to the bar. He said, "Something, Inspector?" in the tone of a man who rather hoped there wouldn't be.

"The man in the dinner jacket," Heimrich said. "And the woman with him. They—didn't wait?"

"They're staying here," Shepley said. "For the night, anyhow. Gave up on the party they were bound for, what with the ice and everything. Name of Barkston. What it looked like, anyway. Signed for their dinner and drinks. Room Two-A. That's the big one on the corner. Went up to it—anyway I guess they did—right after you and your son went up. Said to tell you they'd be around if wanted."

"Yes. When did they get here, Joe?"

"Somewheres around seven, give or take. Asked Mrs. Cushing about a room. Said they were going to 'give up on it.' Way he put it. And could they use the telephone. Mrs. Cushing said of course they could. He used the one on the bar."

"You hear what he said?"

"Couldn't help hearing. Lot of people here by then, all talking. About what a lousy night it was, and whether their plumbing would freeze, mostly. Mr. Barkston, if that's what his name is, had to speak sorta loud."

"Yes, Joe. Happen to hear who he was speaking to?"

"Somebody named Amelia, way I got it. Told her where they were and that they didn't think they could make it. Said something like, 'We'd need a tank, dear, and we haven't even got chains.' Something like that. And that they were sorry as hell to miss the party. Then he said, 'Just candles, dear?' and something about it's being a lousy break for everybody. Then he hung up and wanted to know if I knew how to make stingers."

"And did you, Joe?"

"Sure. Hate to have to drink them myself, but I can make them. Each of them had two rounds before dinner. Wanted something called duck à l'orange, Lucy says. She told them we didn't run to that and they settled for roast beef. Wanted crepes suzettes for desserts and settled for apple pie. People from the city, I guess."

Heimrich said he supposed so, and thought briefly of the *canard rôti à l'orange* he and Susan had had the summer before at the Gritti Palace in Venice and of the Soave Bolla they drank with it. He brought his mind back, sternly.

He said, "Mr. Jackson got killed tonight. I suppose you know about that?"

"Yeah, lugged him in, Inspector. Me and the Purvis kid. Smashed up bad, he was. And one hell of a nice guy, old Mr. Jackson was."

"Yes, he was a nice guy, Joe. This evening when he came in and sat over there, by himself." He indicated "over there" with a gesture. "He often came in here alone for dinner?"

"Pretty often. Way I get it, he sleeps over in his office every now and then. Specially in bad weather. His house is hell and gone from here. And nobody to go home to since his wife died."

Heimrich knew where Sam Jackson's house was—a long narrow stretch of gravel road off Van Brunt Pass—and that it was not a house anybody would elect to drive to on an icy night. He also knew that Jackson had been a widower for more than ten years; had been a widower before Heimrich had first met him.

"Tonight, Joe. Happen to notice who went out just before Mr. Jackson did? Maybe a quarter of an hour before—maybe half an hour?"

"No, can't say I do, Inspector. Not to name anybody. Pretty busy tonight from, oh, about half-past six on. Started to come in when it began to ice up. Even before the electricity went off. Knew it was going to, like always. Goddamn power company must stick them up with old chewing gum. The wires, I mean."

"Yes, Joe. When, about, did Mr. Jackson go out, would you say?"

"About half an hour, maybe, after you and Mrs. Heimrich left, I'd say. Didn't notice specially. We were still pretty busy. Lucy took him over a couple of brandies, and more coffee, I guess."

"He was alone at the table all the time?"

"Pretty much, I guess. Just sitting there by himself. But, like I say, we were still sorta busy. I don't remember anybody stopping by his table, but somebody could of, I guess. You see, Inspector, I didn't know he was going to get himself killed. So there was no reason to keep watching him, was there?"

"No, Joe. Nobody knew he was going to get himself killed."

Except for the driver, sex uncertain, of a big station wagon, make unknown, waiting in a parking lot.

Heimrich turned with his back to the bar, facing those still sitting in the barroom, still waiting out the storm. Heimrich knew most of them; most of them were, to some degree, neighbors. Heimrich could assume all of them—about a dozen now, mostly in pairs—knew what had happened. He told them, anyway. Sam Jackson had been knocked down and killed while he was crossing the parking lot, presumably on his way back to his office on the other side of Van Brunt Avenue.

"Apparently," he said, "somebody backed out without looking. Backed into Mr. Jackson. Didn't report what had happened. Maybe didn't even know he'd hit anybody." (It was a version. There was no point in making it hard for people; in asking them to, possibly, betray a friend.) "Chances are it was somebody who'd been here and decided he could make it home. The point is, did any of you notice who went out before Sam did? Ten minutes before? Maybe longer than that before? Could be he had trouble getting his engine running. Had it going just when Sam went out."

They all looked at him, and there was nothing Heimrich could see in any of the faces turned toward him. Most of them shook their heads. For a minute or so, nobody said anything. Then Bill Aldridge, first vice-president of the Van Brunt First National Bank and Trust Company, said, "Damn shame. Great old guy, Sam was. We counted a lot on old Sam. He was the lawyer for the bank, y'know, M.L. Had been for years. Back to the time old Orville ran things there."

"Yes," Heimrich said, "Sam was a swell guy." Orville, for which read Orville Phipps, hadn't been. He had got himself killed, more or less because he wasn't.

"A loss to the community," Roy Perkins said. "An irreparable loss." He had a just perceptible difficulty with "irreparable." He might, Heimrich thought, have even more difficulty driving on the ice outside.

With it started, half a dozen more paid tribute to the memory of that swell guy, Samuel Jackson. But nobody could put a name to anyone who had left the taproom a few minutes before Jackson had gone out. Somebody thought maybe the Kramers had. But somebody else was pretty sure Robert and Alice Kramer had left much earlier. A few minutes after eight, the somebody thought. Kramer had said to his wife that things weren't going to get any better and that they might as well have a crack at it.

"Anybody know what kind of car hit him?" Aldridge wanted to know. "Anybody see it happen?"

"Seems to have been a station wagon," Heimrich said, and let it lie there.

"Not the Kramers, then," Aldridge said. "They've got a little Chevy." He didn't add that he knew because the bank was financing the little Chevy. He didn't particularly need to.

"All right," Heimrich said, when tributes had all been paid, or agreed with by nodding heads. "No reason to keep you people here any longer. If any of you remember anything that might help, let me know."

Heads nodded again, but nobody showed any immediate intention of venturing out onto the ice. It was a night to postpone.

Suddenly, there was the sound of a siren outside. It was hitting the interrupted notes of an ambulance siren. Then there were sounds from the lobby, and a dozen heads turned in the direction of the sounds. Somebody in the lobby said, "Got it?" and some other man said, "Yeah," and then, "Sure mashed him up, didn't it?" Nobody answered that, and they could hear the outside lobby door close.

One couple stood up and the man got heavy coats off a rack and they put the coats on. The show was over. Exit victim; exit audience. Others got coats.

Before any of them reached the door to the parking lot, the door opened and a trooper in uniform came in. Just inside the door he stopped and, more or less, came to attention.

Before he spoke, Heimrich said, "Evening, Purvis."

Corporal Asa Purvis, New York State Police, said, "Inspector, sir." Purvis was a stickler for formality. He somewhat spoiled it by adding, "Sure is a lousy one, isn't it?" Nobody quarreled with that.

"They haven't got hold of Lieutenant Forniss, Inspector," Purvis said. "Still trying. Too damn bad about Mr. Jackson."

Heimrich agreed it was too bad about Mr. Jackson. He said, "Glad it was you on tonight, Asa. Could be it's a lucky break."

Purvis said "Sir" with a suggestion of inquiry in the word.

"Come along inside," Heimrich said, and led the way into the lobby. Mary Cushing was behind the desk. She was sorting checks. There were two chairs in the small lobby, in addition to the now-empty sofa. There was a bloodstain at one end of the sofa. Heimrich sat in one of the chairs, and gestured Purvis toward the other.

"We're looking for a station wagon," Heimrich said. "A big one, apparently. Probably dark-colored. The one that ran over Mr. Jackson. Can you think of a likely one, Asa?"

"It's pretty vague, Inspector. We don't know the make?"

They didn't know the make.

"Just generally," Purvis said, "there could be twenty around here. You mean here in the village, sir?"

"Anywhere around here, I'm afraid."

"Could be a hundred, counting in Cold Harbor," Purvis said. "Could be twice that, sir. Damn near everybody around here's got a wagon. Almost as many as've got a Volks. Dad must service about a dozen. Wagons, I mean."

Asa's father owns PURVIS'S GARAGE, TWENTY-FOUR-HOUR WRECKING SERVICE. And also gas and oil and tire service. Tune-ups a specialty.

"He'll have a list of the owners," Heimrich said. He said it as a statement, but Asa Purvis said, "Sure," and then added, "Yes, Inspector, sir."

"Somebody may bring a wagon in for service tomorrow," Heimrich said. "Banged-up rear end, could be. Maybe even tonight, but I doubt it. Probably early tomorrow, when the roads thaw off. If they do."

"Rain's letting up," Purvis said. "Get some sun tomorrow and the roads ought to be all right. Except where trees have fallen on them. Couple of big branches down on the road between here and Cold Harbor, but you can get around them. Won't do anybody much good to go around tonight. Both the wreckers out. Saw that when I came through. Dad's probably on one of them."

It was, of course, a night for wrecking trucks to be attending wrecks. And for Jeremiah Purvis to be on one of them, although Jeremiah was well into his sixties.

"Yes, Asa, probably wait till morning. If a banged-up wagon shows, we'll want to know where it was last night. And who was driving it, naturally." He paused. Should he have Corporal Purvis stay at the inn overnight? On the second floor, outside the rooms occupied by Joan Collins and Michael Faye? Just in case? Maybe.

"Tell you what, Corporal, suppose you scout around outside and see what you can find. A car starting up, or back, suddenly—a car with chains on it—would tear up the ice some. Got a camera in the cruiser?"

"Yes, Inspector."

"Might get shots of anything you think would interest us. Scraped ice, before it freezes smooth again. Bloodstains and distances. Anything that might help a jury get the picture, O.K.? When you get that done, you might make a list of people around here who own big wagons. Go up to the garage, if you need to, and go through your dad's records. Then come back here. Right?"

"Yes, sir."

They went out into the taproom. One couple was still there, with coffee and cognac glasses in front of them. They were both young; both, evidently, filled with the confidence of youth, the confidence that bad things, like sliding off roads into trees, only happen to other people. Particularly, of course, to older other people.

Heimrich watched Asa Purvis go out of the taproom toward the parking lot. He got up and crossed to the inn's desk. Mary Cushing was putting a rubber band around a packet of dinner checks. She finished that and looked up at Heimrich.

"Michael and Miss Collins seem to be all right, M.L.," Mary said. "She seemed about ready to go to sleep when I came down. And Michael was going into his own room. At least, he said he was. I mean——"

"Yes, Mary, I know what you mean. Probably left the door open a little so he could hear her if she wanted anything."

"She seems like a nice girl," Mary Cushing said. "Awful thing to happen to her, wasn't it?"

"Yes, Mary. And Susan and I like her, too. Many people staying overnight here?"

"Just Michael and Miss Collins and a couple from the city. On their way to a party, they say, and decided to give it up. Name of Barkston, Mr. and Mrs. Clement Barkston. And maybe those kids out in the taproom, if they ever make up their minds. The boy came in and asked about a room, and said they'd let me know." She looked at the watch on her wrist. "About time they did," she said. "He did say him and his wife, M.L. But I don't—" She let it trail off.

"All you can know is what they tell you," Heimrich said. "And I'm not vice squad, Mary. About the Barkstons. Happen to notice if they left the taproom at any point while I was at home? To get something they'd forgotten out of their car? That sort of thing?"

"Not that I saw. But I wasn't around all the time. Had to go out to the kitchen to tell Leon we looked like having a late night. He yelled at me, the way he always does. Cooks who call themselves chefs!"

Heimrich made sounds he hoped were consoling.

"And then I went up to Miss Collins, of course."

"Tough on the Barkstons," Heimrich said. "All dressed up to go to a party, and no way—no safe way, anyhow—to get there. A dress-up party, apparently."

"Amelia Lord's, M.L. Asked me if I thought they could make it, and I had to tell them it would be bad going, the Lord house being on the top of a hill and all. Bad break for Mrs. Lord, too. First party she's had since——"

"Yes," Heimrich said. "Since her husband was killed last summer."

"That's right. Since that Kemper woman shot him. They used to give a lot of parties, way I get it. We catered one of them. Must have been fifty people at it. Theater people, most of them. Anyway, they acted like it."

Heimrich did not ask how "theater people" acted. He knew Mary Cushing well enough to know she was as conventional as her overdone meat. But, also, the late Burton Lord had been a theatrical producer, and a very successful one. His parties might have been expected to attract people of the theater.

"That couple out there," Mary said. "They'd better make up their minds if they're ever going to. I'm going to tell Joe to close the bar. And tell them if they want a room they'll have to register and go take it. Don't they know people have to sleep? Even people who run inns? What do they think we are?"

Heimrich did not hazard an answer. "People who have elected to supply other people with food and lodging" might have been an answer. It was one there was no point in making. Heimrich said he wouldn't know. His tone agreed that people are unreasonable. He said, "Like to use your telephone, Mary."

He used the telephone to call the barracks. He told the duty sergeant to give up on Lieutenant Forniss for the night; in the morning ask the Lieutenant to come down to Van Brunt, to the Old Stone Inn. "I'll join him there. Tell him about nine will be all right."

Mary Cushing was going into the taproom when Heimrich turned from the telephone. Probably, he thought, to tell the young couple to make up their minds. And Joe Shepley to close the bar. He sat down again to wait for young Purvis, so vigilantly a corporal of the state police.

The couple who had lingered in the taproom came out of it into the lobby, and Mrs. Cushing came with them. She went behind the desk and they stood in front of it and registered. She said, "Two-B. Just turn left at the top of the stairs. I'm afraid there isn't anybody to help with your bag. We usually close earlier. The boy's off now."

"Perfectly all right," the young man said. "We realize this hasn't been a usual evening. You do serve breakfast?"

"From eight to nine thirty," Mary said. "Here's your key, Mr. Jones." She put a just perceptible emphasis on the word "Jones." It was clear to Heimrich that Mary Cushing still had her doubts. But a good many people are named Jones. Some are named Doe, come to that.

The couple went up the stairs, the man carrying a single light overnight case, the girl only a large handbag.

Mary said, "Well?"

"Nothing more tonight," Heimrich said. "I'll just wait for the Corporal. You better turn in, Mary. I'll be back in the morning, probably. But nothing more tonight."

Mary said, "All right, Inspector," making it formal, and went up the stairs.

Young Purvis was taking his time about it, Heimrich thought. A very thorough boy, Purvis. Probably planned to end up as head of the New York State Police. Or of the FBI, possibly.

Heimrich heard footfalls from the taproom. At last. Should he leave Purvis to keep an eye on things for the rest of the night? He still hadn't made up his mind. Almost certainly there was no real need to. Send him back to the substation. The state police would need all the troopers they could lay hands on, a night like this.

It was not Asa Purvis who came into the lobby from the taproom. It was Joe Shepley. He was carrying a tray with a bottle on it and two small brandy snifters.

"Thought you'd closed for the night, Joe," Heimrich said.

"Have, Inspector. But the people who were going to a party decided they needed a nightcap and phoned down for it. Martell, he said, and to bring the bottle."

He started up the stairs.

"As long as they're still up," Heimrich said, "I may as well have a word with them."

He followed the barman up the stairs.

Barkston had loosened the collar of his soft dress shirt, a moderately pleated dress shirt. His wife was sitting by the fire in a softly green robe.

Barkston opened the door. He said, "Right over there, if you will." He indicated a table next to his wife's chair. Then he looked at Heimrich and raised his eyebrows.

"Inspector Heimrich, state police," Heimrich told him. "Only keep you a minute or so. About what happened here tonight. As long as you're both still up."

Clement Barkston was, at a guess, in his late fifties. He was somewhat stocky; his gray hair was rather long and had been styled with care. He merely nodded his head toward Heimrich. He watched Joe put the tray on the table. He said, "Thank you," and signed the check Joe gave him. He put two dollar bills on the check and handed the money and the check to the barman. He said, "Sorry to bother you. You were probably just closing up."

Joe said, "Thank *you*, sir, no bother at all, sir," and went out of the room.

Barkston said, "Yes, Inspector? Care to join us? I can get a glass from the bathroom."

Heimrich said, "No, thanks, Mr. Barkston. Just one or two minor points. About Mr. Jackson's death."

Barkston had supposed it would be that. The boy who'd brought their bags up had said something about it. But they didn't know anything about it.

"We were just going to a party," Mrs. Barkston said. "But it got so bad we began to wonder. There didn't seem to be lights on anywhere but here. So we stopped. We thought somebody might know how things were on up."

"And were told they were worse, if anything," her husband said. "And decided to give the party up and stay overnight. Came up rather early. Missed the whole thing, actually."

"And glad to," Mrs. Barkston said, and half turned to face Heimrich. "Beautiful" would be the word for her, Heimrich thought. Younger than her husband, but probably only by a few years. But still beautiful. And, somehow, a little familiar. Heimrich felt he might have seen her before. Or seen a picture of her. Then it seeped into his mind—Elaine Bentley. Several years before he had seen her acting at a theater on 45th Street. He and Susan had seen the play together. Her name had been in lights above the name of the play. "Elaine Bentley in——" He couldn't remember in what. It hadn't mattered much. Elaine Bentley had mattered a lot. They had both agreed on that.

When he is working, Merton Heimrich's face is usually unrevealing. There is no comment visible on it to the answers he gets to questions; none when he asks the questions. Neutrality of expression is part of his job. But this time, a little to his surprise, his face had been revealing.

"Yes, Inspector," Elaine Barkston said, and smiled at him. There was great warmth in her smile. "I am. Used to be, anyway. And it's pleasant to be remembered, Inspector. You get to feeling that everybody has forgotten. Wondering, really, if anybody ever knew."

"Yes, Miss Bentley," Heimrich said. "People knew. And I'm sure thousands remember."

She said, "Thank you. You're a darling, really."

Heimrich tried to adjust his mind to this new role as "darling." He became conscious that he was smiling widely at the woman in front of the fire—smiling idiotically, no doubt.

Barkston crossed the room—the large room; Mary Cushing had provided her best for them. Responding, Heimrich supposed, to a dinner jacket and an evening dress. Barkston joined his wife in front of the fire. He poured into the brandy snifters. He looked up at Heimrich and said, "Sure you won't?" and, when Heimrich shook his head, "You wanted to ask us questions?"

"Only a few. Mr. Jackson was hit by a car in the parking lot. Possibly by someone who had just gone out from the bar and was on his or her way home. Mr. Jackson was a tall, rather thin man. He was sitting at a table near the wall. By himself, far as we can learn. He had gray hair. Was wearing a dark business suit. Either of you happen to notice him?"

"I did," Elaine Barkston said. "He looked sort of—lonely, I thought. But a good many people seemed to know him. And he did stop at your table, didn't he? It looked, oh, like a family group. Then a very pretty child with long hair came in. Your daughter, Inspector?"

"No. A friend of my son's. You thought Jackson looked lonely, Mrs. Barkston?"

"If I wanted to look lonely, waiting for somebody who didn't come, I'd have looked the way he did. Tried to, anyway. But perhaps he always looked that way."

Sam Jackson hadn't, but it was nothing that needed going into.

"Did either of you notice somebody going out just before he did?"

"Can't help you there, I'm afraid," Barkston said. "He was still sitting there when Elly and I came up. Wasn't he, dear?"

"Yes, I'm sure he was. Sitting there and drinking coffee and looking disconsolate. But maybe I'm just imagining that, Inspector. Not that he was still there. But the way he looked. I do imagine things, I'm afraid. Make up scenes to go with expressions. Facial expressions, I mean."

"Yes, dear," Barkston said. "Look, Inspector, from the way you go about this, I take it this wasn't just a traffic accident? You seem to be implying that somebody went out of the bar and got into a car and waited for this man Jackson to come out so he could be run over. Is that what you think happened?"

"We think it's a possibility," Heimrich said. "We try to look into all possibilities. After you came up here, to your room, you didn't have occasion to go down again? To get something you'd forgotten out of your car, maybe? My wife and I often have to do that."

"No, we came up here and stayed here. Didn't go down to the car and run anybody over. Just sat here and talked about poor Amelia's party, which probably was a washout. Iceout, really. And decided to have cognac sent up. And you came with it, didn't you?"

"Yes," Heimrich said. "What kind of car is yours, by the way?"

"Mercedes, Inspector. And it's right down there, getting ice all over it. You can always look at it and see if it's got dents in it from hitting a man. Somebody see a man get hit by a Mercedes?"

"No, Mr. Barkston. Seems like the car that killed Mr. Jackson was a station wagon. Have your drinks. The ice probably will have melted off the roads by tomorrow."

"You mean we can go back to town? That you won't want to ask us more questions?"

"I shouldn't think so, Mr. Barkston. Not in what people call the foreseeable future." He started for the door and stopped and turned back. "You're not acting anymore, Mrs. Barkston? The theater must miss you."

"No," she said. "I'm retired for good. The theater will make do, I suspect. And you're really a sweet man, Inspector."

Heimrich went then. Corporal Purvis was waiting in the lobby. He had got pictures. "You were right about the car having torn up the ice, Inspector. Looks as if the car—well, just jumped backward. Chains really ripped the ice up."

The taproom was dim, all lights off except one over the bar. Joe Shepley was washing glasses.

Yes, Samuel Jackson often came to the inn in the evenings. Two or three times a week, actually. Sometimes just for a drink; sometimes for dinner. You could, Joe guessed, pretty much call him a regular customer. Particularly in the winter when the weather was bad. "He lives to hell and gone, Inspector."

So did Heimrich. He told Purvis to check with his father about big, dark-colored station wagons and to get a list together of people who owned them and come to the inn with it in the morning.

Heimrich went out to the Buick. The rain had stopped, finally. The wind was as strong as before. But now it was coming from the northwest. You could see the sky, now. There seemed even to be a few holes in the clouds.

Chapter 5

The sun came up late, which was in accord with the calendar; it came up bright, in accord with the forecast of the U.S. Weather Service. The Heimrichs got the forecast, dimly, on a battery radio. *The New York Times*, that Tuesday morning, the day before Christmas, did not come up at all. The boy who delivered it to the house above the Hudson, must have been iced in like everybody else.

It had not been a restful night for Susan and Merton Heimrich. Sleeping with clothes on on a mattress in front of a log fire which needs frequent replenishment is not a comfortable way to sleep. Heimrich had slept in snatches, between putting more logs on. Once he had had to go out into the breezeway to wrench logs from the frozen pile. It was no longer a galeway, with the shift of the wind to the northwest; it was no longer wet. It was, however, even more slippery underfoot. The iced logs sizzled disconsolately before, finally, they caught. But, by then, only scattered clouds hurried across the sky.

The fumes from the oil stove hadn't been conducive to sleep. Nor had the oil stove done much to warm the kitchen. The small teakettle of water, still warmish from the last gasps of the water heater, was still not much more than warmish from its night on top of the oil stove. That led to warmish instant coffee. And bread could be toasted at the fire.

"I could warm us eggs, I suppose," Susan said. "Do we want faintly warmed eggs?"

The decision was against faintly warmed eggs. It was for brief, and chilling, face washing in cold water. (There was still water in the pressure tank; there was no telling how much. There was enough water to flush toilets—this once, anyway.)

"We'll both go to the inn for breakfast," Heimrich said, and was firm about it. "Tell you what, we'll take a room there. A room with bath."

"And come back every half hour or so to keep the fire going."

"And come back every hour or so to keep the fire going," Merton agreed. "The sun will warm things up a little."

He went to the window and looked at the thermometer. It was covered with ice. Finally, he located the mercury column. It showed twenty-five. Unless, of course, it was showing fifteen. Susan fed Mite, who had been talking about it, and Colonel, who was too depressed to say anything, but who consented to eat. They put more logs on the fire. Heimrich got the can of kerosene from the garage and refilled—and then relighted—the fuming stove. They went out into the sunlight.

And a million tiny suns dazzled their eyes. Each smallest twig, each pine needle, sparkled at them. This was true as far as they could see. The whole world glittered.

"It's beautiful, isn't it?" Susan said. "How can anything so beautiful be so ugly?"

Heimrich, who was backing the Buick to face it down the drive —and discovering that the sun still hadn't had time or strength to melt the ice, and thinking that fifteen had probably been right on the thermometer—said "Mmm." But the "mm" was appreciative.

On Van Brunt Avenue, even the low slanting sun, helped by sand and the modicum of salt mixed with it, had begun to melt the pavement ice. Once they had skidded down to it, making the Old Stone Inn wasn't bad—not if you stayed at twenty. The parking lot was still glazed, but one of the Purvis boys—Jeremiah, Junior, or Jacob?—was tossing rock salt on it. There were three cars in the lot and one of them was a state police cruiser. They went into the tap-room. There was a fire in the room. There was nobody behind the bar. Corporal Asa Purvis and Lieutenant Charles Forniss were sitting at a table near the fire. Both were drinking coffee.

Susan said, "Good morning, Charles. Hi, Asa," and, to Heimrich, "I'll go see Mary about a room. With bath. For periodic use. And I'll see about breakfast."

She went into the lobby.

Heimrich said, "Morning, Charlie. Corporal."

Asa Purvis stood up, more or less at attention. He said, "Sir." (Young Purvis could, on occasion, be a little trying.) Forniss said, "Morning, M.L. Quite a night, wasn't it? People sliding into trees all over the place."

"Here, into other people," Heimrich told him and joined them at the table. He said, "Oh, sit down, Asa," to the still-standing Corporal of the New York State Police. Asa said, "Sir," and sat down. He sat erect, still somewhat at attention.

Heimrich asked him what he had got from his father. Purvis took a typed sheet out of his pocket and looked at it. He handed it to Heimrich. "Seventeen wagons pretty regularly," Asa said. "All kinds, seems like."

Reading the list of owners, license numbers, and makes of station wagons, Heimrich nodded his head. "All kinds" was right—Pontiacs and Oldses, a variety of Fords, Chryslers under several model names, an American Motors or two. One Cadillac, which was a mild surprise. Heimrich hadn't known Cadillac made a station wagon. Probably a special job for—for Farmington Crothers. Well, Crothers could afford to have a Cadillac made to his preference. Probably a Rolls, come to that.

All but one of the cars carried Putnam County plates. The exception had a "V" prefix. (Which, Arnold Goldberg had once assured Heimrich, stood for "Vestchester.") The names of most of the owners were known to Inspector Heimrich. They told him nothing. Oh, he rather doubted that the Reverend Dr. Francis Armstrong had backed his 1970 Pontiac wagon into Samuel Jackson and then reversed it to run Sam Jackson over.

"None of these been in for repairs?" Heimrich asked Asa Purvis.

None had. "Nobody had been in for anything, when I stopped by," Asa said, and added "Sir" to make it official. "Things are still pretty much iced up, Inspector."

Forniss said they sure as hell were. He said that all the cruisers operating out of the barracks were still wearing chains. "But the generator's working O.K.," he added.

The morning waitress came in through the lobby from the dining room. She carried a tray with a coffeepot on it, and a cup and a small pitcher of cream and some packets of sugar. She said, "Good morning, sir. Mrs. Heimrich said to bring this in. And she's ordered breakfast, sir. And she says you'd better have some too, Inspector. She said, 'Tell him that's an order.'"

Steam was coming from the spout of the coffeepot. Fragrance was coming, too. The lukewarm instant at home hadn't smelled of anything. Or tasted of it, either.

"Tell her to go ahead," Heimrich said. "Tell her I'll be along." He poured himself coffee. It steamed in the cup. He added cream.

"Mrs. Heimrich says will soft-boiled eggs be all right," the waitress said.

"Tell her I'll be along in a few minutes," Heimrich said. "Only, don't let them put the eggs in yet."

"And bacon? She said to ask you about bacon."

"All right, bacon," Heimrich said. "In—oh, about fifteen minutes. Tell Mrs. Heimrich I'll be in."

The waitress said, "Thank you, sir," and went back where she had come from. Heimrich drank coffee.

"Corporal's filled me in," Forniss said. "Could be it's just vehicular homicide, couldn't it? Just some damn fool not looking where he was going?"

"He told you about Miss Collins, Charlie? What it looked like to her?"

"Yeah. Only, I take it she's a kid pretty much. And probably tired as hell after that drive down from Hanover. Tired kids—all kids, sometimes—see things that aren't there. Imagine things, if you know what I mean, M.L. Get—oh, worked up."

"Yes," Heimrich said, "we both know that happens. And not only with kids, Charles. And Miss Collins isn't that much of a kid and I don't think she was that tired. I've talked to her. I don't think she's hallucinating. She may have been wrong, of course. But I think she saw what she says she saw. And if she did, it's murder one."

Charles Forniss said "Mmm." He said, "I didn't know Mr. Jackson except to say hello to. He seemed like a nice old guy. Why'd anybody want to kill him? Figure he was mixed up in something?"

"He was a nice guy," Heimrich said. "I don't know what he was mixed up in, except drawing wills and making out contracts and things like that. And handling legal matters for the bank."

"Foreclosures, maybe? Can make people sore, being foreclosed."

Heimrich said he didn't know, and that they'd have to try and find out, wouldn't they? He finished his coffee. He felt it dissolving morning grumpiness. He poured himself another cup and drank it quickly. He stood up.

"Don't forget you're supposed to have breakfast, M.L.," Forniss said, as one friend to another. "Susan'll be upset if you forget."

"O.K.," Heimrich said. "O.K. You've had yours?"

"At the barracks."

"All right. Jackson had a secretary. A Miss Arnold, I think she is. Maybe she'll show up at his office, and maybe she won't. Try to get in touch with her, Charlie. Tell her we'd like to talk to her in—oh, about half an hour. At Jackson's if that's all right with her. I'll go eat those damn eggs."

Breakfast is not Heimrich's favorite meal. Also, he thinks he weighs at least enough. He is wont to think of himself as resembling a hippopotamus. He went through the lobby into the inn's dining room.

Susan was alone in the dining room. She was alone at a table for four. She was smoking a cigarette and drinking coffee.

"I ordered for you," she said. "Soft-boiled eggs and bacon and coffee. The kids are having breakfast in their rooms, Mary says.

Special dispensation. She had to tell some people named Barkston the inn doesn't run to room service. Mary's talkative this morning."

Heimrich said "Mmm" and helped himself to coffee from Susan's pot.

"It'll be cold," Susan said. "They're bringing you fresh."

Susan was right. And they did bring him fresh, with the bacon and eggs. The eggs were, as Heimrich had expected, almost hard-boiled. He ate them anyway. He also ate his bacon. He even ate most of a piece of toast. Susan watched him approvingly. When he had lighted a cigarette, she said, "And now, dear?"

Heimrich raised his eyebrows.

"And now, what do we do, dear? Drive Joan back to the house to get her car? So she can go on to New York and spend Christmas with a father who climbs walls?"

Heimrich drew deeply on his cigarette. He poured himself more coffee. Susan waited. He sipped from his refilled cup and, again, inhaled deeply. Finally, he said, "I suppose so. Suppose we have to. Only—" He stopped speaking and looked over his wife's head at the ceiling. Again Susan waited.

"Only," he said, "I'd like her to stay around for a while. Maybe look at a few station wagons. Go over what she saw a couple of times, maybe. But I don't like to make Mr. Collins climb walls."

He drank coffee. He said, "Tell you what, Susan. Suppose you ask her to stay around for a day or two. Or urge her to drive to New York and pluck her father from whatever wall he's climbing and then come back here. Tell her it's just a request. That she can go in if she really feels she has to. All right?"

Susan supposed it was all right. She did say, "Why me?"

"Because I've got to try to find out who killed Sam," Merton told her.

"Poor dear, Sam," Susan said. "He never hurt anybody, did he? Why this—this awful thing?"

"I don't know, dear. We'll try to find out."

"It wasn't just an accident, Merton?"

"It could have been, yes. But from what the girl saw—" He finished with a shrug of his shoulders. "She seems a bright girl, Michael's Joan."

"Yes. And you want her here so—so that you can keep an eye on her. See that nothing happens to her. That's it, isn't it? Not to look at station wagons."

Heimrich finished his coffee. He stood up.

"All right," he said. "That does enter in. There's a chance somebody may think she saw more than she did see. Or remembers seeing. But don't tell her that, dear. Just try to persuade her to call her father and tell him she's dreadfully sorry, but she's held up. Or whatever she wants to tell him. That she'll be home for New Year's Eve, or whatever."

He looked down at his wife, who smiled and nodded her head.

"I'll try, Merton," Susan said. "And then go back to the house and tend the fire. And try to pacify the animals. You won't need the car?"

"Charlie's got a car. Then come back here for lunch. O.K.?"

"Yes. About one?"

They agreed on about one, give or take. It was Susan who interpolated the "give or take." She is familiar with the uncertainty of a policeman's hours.

She lighted another cigarette after she had watched her tall husband walk to the lobby and through it. Even when he's just walking it's as if he were dancing, Susan thought. Merton Heimrich does not remind his wife of a hippopotamus.

Joan Collins and Michael were coming down the stairs when Heimrich walked through the lobby. They looked to be all right. He said "Good morning" to them and went on toward the taproom. He stopped and turned back. "Your mother's in the dining room," he said. "Wants to be sure you're both all right." Then he went on.

It had been a foolish thing to say, he thought. There was no reason they shouldn't be all right—no *real* reason.

Both Charles Forniss and Asa Purvis stood up this time when Heimrich went in. Asa stood straighter. Also, Asa was not smoking. There was no rule against smoking while on duty, except in Asa Purvis's perhaps overdedicated mind. Forniss did grind out his cigarette.

"All set with Miss Arnold," Forniss said. "She's waiting for us at the office. First name's Alice. She sounded upset as hell on the phone. And can't think of anything she can tell us about this terrible accident."

"Maybe there won't be," Heimrich said. "But we'll have to see, won't we? Corporal!"

Asa Purvis stood even straighter as he said, "Sir!"

"What I want you to do is to drive around and look at station wagons," Heimrich told him. "You've got your father's list?"

"No, sir," Purvis told him. "You've got it, Inspector. I gave——"

Heimrich said, "Of course, Asa," and took out of his pocket the typed list of station wagons regularly serviced by Purvis's Garage at The Corners. He gave it to Asa. He said, "You know what to look for?"

"Yes, sir. Dents. And blood on tire chains, any that have chains. And try to find out whether any of them was being driven last night. That right, sir?"

There was the faintest possible suggestion of reproach in young Purvis's voice. It belonged there, Heimrich thought. Coffee had not entirely dissolved the morning grumpiness. You don't tell a good cop to do the obvious. And Asa was shaping into a very good cop. Heimrich ought to say he was sorry. He said, "You're entirely right, Asa. We'll be at Mr. Jackson's office for a while, if you turn up anything."

They went out of the taproom into the glittering sunlight. Sun and salt had melted the ice from the parking lot, although it was still cold and the wind still blustering. Purvis went to his squad car. He drove out ahead of Heimrich and Forniss and turned south on Van Brunt Avenue.

There were still icy spots on N.Y. 11-F as they walked across it—spots evergreens had shaded. But most of the pavement was free of ice, and drying. Traffic was having no problems. They had to wait to cross through it.

Samuel Jackson's office was on the second floor of a venerable white house, set back some fifty feet from the avenue and a hundred yards or so nearer The Corners than the Old Stone Inn. The Walthrop Insurance Agency occupied the ground floor. They climbed stairs. The door at the top of them had a ground glass panel with "Samuel Jackson, Attorney and Counselor-at-Law" lettered on it.

They opened the door and went into Sam Jackson's outer office, an office Jackson would never again walk through. It was a small room, on the avenue side of the old house—a house which had been somebody's "mansion" when N.Y. 11-F was a dirt road, probably, and certainly a road without a number. It was a rather dark, small room; the sun was still hours from its west-facing windows.

The woman sitting at the desk facing the door was not looking at the door. She jumped in her chair when she heard the door open, and then turned to face them. Her movement was almost convulsive. She had been looking out one of the windows at the street; looking fixedly at the traffic moving on Van Brunt Avenue. Looking without seeing. And she had, Heimrich thought, been crying.

She was, he guessed, in her late forties or early fifties. Her grayish blond hair was set in ripples. Her chin quivered a little. She was a small, neat woman, and when she spoke it was in a small, neat voice, which quavered.

She said, "I'm afraid Mr. Jackson—" and did not go on. She merely looked at them. Her small mouth twitched.

Heimrich said, "Miss Arnold?" and she nodded her head. She spoke again, and this time her voice was steadier.

"I'm afraid Mr. Jackson can't—" she said, and again did not finish. Heimrich told her who they were and she said, "Oh." The sound shook on her lips. She said, "It's terrible, isn't it? I can't really believe it. He was such—such a fine man. Nobody told me until I got here and I thought—thought he'd stayed overnight in his office, because it was such an awful night. He does sometimes when the weather's bad. I thought perhaps he was still asleep, although he's usually here before I am. Then I thought, perhaps he's decided to take the day off because it's Christmas Eve. Then the telephone rang and—" Her voice broke.

They waited. Her eyes filled, and she got tissue out of her desk drawer and dabbed them.

"It was Mrs. Cushing at the inn," she said. "She told me what had happened—the terrible thing that has happened. Right across the street. The terrible accident to Mr. Jackson. That's why you're here, isn't it? You're trying to find out how the accident happened. I was home by then. So I don't know anything about it, except Mrs. Cushing said he was run over by a car. Right in the parking lot."

She shivered. She said, "I'm sorry. It's terribly cold in here, isn't it?"

It was cold in the little room—the room the sun wouldn't reach until midafternoon.

"Yes, it is, Miss Arnold," Heimrich agreed. "Perhaps we'd better go into Mr. Jackson's office. The sun ought to be coming in there, oughtn't it?"

"I can't tell you anything, Inspector. And I don't know——"

"Mr. Jackson was a friend of mine," Heimrich said. "Had been a friend for years. He'd want you to help us any way you can. We do have a few questions we'd like to ask you. Perhaps we'd better go into his office."

She said, "Well, I guess it'll be all right."

She still didn't seem at all certain it would be, but she got up from her desk and went ahead of them to a closed door. She opened the door and they followed her down a rather long, and very dim, corridor, to a door at the end of it. She opened that door, and they went after her into a large room and a bright one. Morning sunlight streamed into it through two floor-to-ceiling windows. There was a big desk in front of the windows. There were two telephones on the desk and an Aladdin lamp, not lighted. It looked as if Sam Jackson had been working at his desk after dark the evening before. And he had been forearmed against the vagaries of country electricity.

There was nothing on the desk to show at what he had been working.

A fire was laid in a fireplace in one wall of the big room. It was warmer in the big office than it had been in the outer office, but it wasn't all that warm. The sun in late December is a wan sun.

"I suppose," Alice Arnold said, "I could light the fire. Do you think it would be all right if I lighted the fire? I don't think he'll mind, do you?"

The present tense is hard to drop.

"I'm sure he wouldn't," Heimrich told her.

She said "Oh" and got a match from a box of kitchen matches hidden in a ceramic container on a table. She put the match to paper under kindling and logs. The fire started eagerly. There was a stenographer's chair at one end of the big desk and she moved it closer to the fire and sat on it. She sat erect, as if about to take dictation. She looked back at the desk, as if Samuel Jackson, Attorney-at-Law, were behind it and about to ask her to take a letter. Then she looked at the fire and held her hands out toward it. The outstretched hands trembled.

It wasn't warm in the big room, but it wasn't that cold.

Merton Heimrich looked around the big room. Across from the fireplace there was a convertible sofa-bed. It was a bed at the moment. It had been turned down, ready to be slept in. Sam had expected to come back from dinner and light his ready fire and get into his ready bed. Well, many people plan for a next minute which never comes. It is the task of an Inspector, BCI, to determine why those minutes are not to come.

"I can't tell you anything," Alice Arnold said. "What do you want to ask me about the accident?"

"There's this, Miss Arnold," Heimrich said, "we're not sure it was an accident."

For a moment she merely looked at him, her pale blue eyes wide. Then she said, "I don't know what you mean. Mary Cushing said a car hit him as he was crossing the parking——"

"Yes," Heimrich said. "That's the way it happened. The way Mr. Jackson was killed. Somebody backed a station wagon into him and knocked him down and then—then came back and ran over him. It could have been an accident. And it could have been deliberate. If it was deliberate, Mr. Jackson was murdered, Miss Arnold. Why the Lieutenant and I are here, actually."

He drew it out a bit, to give her the time he thought she needed.

She sat for several seconds and merely looked at him. Then she said "Oh," and for the moment stopped with that. Then she said, "I see, Inspector. But—but Mr. Jackson never did anything to anybody. He was kind to everybody. Gentle with everybody. Who would want—"

She left that unfinished, obviously because it did not need finishing. And Heimrich could not have answered it anyway. He told her he didn't know, that that was one thing they were trying to find out. Who, and a why which might lead to the "who."

"Conceivably," he said, "something that had to do with his law practice?"

She looked astonished. She said, "No, I'm sure it couldn't be. If you mean one of our—I mean, his clients—it just couldn't be. Not possibly."

"Probably not, Miss Arnold. Can you give me some idea about his practice? I know he handled legal matters for the bank, of course."

"Yes," she said. "All civil matters, really. Making out wills for people, arranging contracts. Closings, and that sort of thing. All privileged, you know. Nothing I can talk about, of course. Not even now. You do understand that?"

"Yes, Miss Arnold. Approving contracts for bank loans. Things like that. There hadn't been any change in his practice recently? I mean, well, he hadn't taken on clients of a different kind? Criminal cases, say?"

"None of our clients is a criminal," she said. "I can't think what you mean, Inspector. People like old Miss Gee. Surely you wouldn't call her a criminal."

Heimrich knew old Miss Gee. She was in her nineties. She lived in a large house above the Hudson. Her family had lived there for some generations. Van Gee, the name had once been. A large amount of money went with the large house. Heimrich had no idea how, at the moment, she came into anything.

"No," he said, "I wouldn't think of her as a criminal, Miss Arnold. Why did you happen to mention her?"

"No real reason. It's just because of her I happened to be working so late yesterday. Her will, you know. She was changing it again. She often does. Thinks maybe Cousin Ruth would like to have the old grand piano instead of Cousin Harry, who would really prefer the billiard table. She does it all the time, you know."

Heimrich hadn't known. A grandmother of his had similarly twiddled with her will, although she hadn't had grand pianos or billiard tables to leave anyone. He said "Mmm" and then, "You had to work late yesterday afternoon? Typing Miss Gee's new will?"

"You can call it 'afternoon' if you want to, Inspector. It was more like evening, actually. Night, almost. She wanted to sign it today, Mr. Jackson said, and that he was sorry to keep me so late. Not that I minded. I'd do anything for Mr. Jackson. He is a wonderful man to work for."

"I'm sure he was, Miss Arnold. He was a fine man to know. About how late did you work last evening?"

"Half-past seven anyway. I know it was almost eight when I got home, and I live just around the corner. Of course, the ice made it slower. Driving home, I mean. I finished up and answered the telephone and probably it was a quarter of eight before I locked up and started home."

"Answered the telephone," Heimrich said. "A call for Mr. Jackson, I suppose?"

"Of course. But he'd gone by then. Over to the inn for dinner. He offered to wait until I'd finished and take me with him, but I like to finish what I'm doing and it would still take me about half an hour and I didn't want to hold him up, of course."

She wouldn't, Heimrich thought. Sam Jackson had been a fine man to work for. Perhaps to fall a little in love with. Autumnal romance is by no means unheard of, despite what kids of Michael's age may think. Michael's age and his Joan's. He hoped Susan had been able to persuade the girl not to drive on into the city and pluck her father from whatever wall he was climbing. Not that there was any real reason to worry about Joan Collins.

"This telephone call," he said. "Mind telling me who called, Miss Arnold?"

"I don't know. Whoever it was just wanted to speak to Mr. Jackson. And I said he'd just gone across the street to dinner."

"You didn't ask who was calling?"

"Of course I did. So Mr. Jackson could call back, if it was important. But whoever it was said not to bother. That it wasn't all that important. And hung up."

"Man or woman, Miss Arnold? The one who called?"

"A man, I guess. Only the voice was—oh, a little muffled. As if whoever it was had a cold. But I think it was a man. Oh, and something you asked me about a few minutes ago. About anything different recently in Mr. Jackson's practice. There was——"

But then the telephone rang, and she went to Jackson's big desk to answer it.

Chapter 6

She said, "Mr. Jackson's office, good morning, may I—" and stopped. She said, "Oh, yes, he is. Just a—" But by that time Heimrich was beside her and holding out his hand for the receiver. He spoke his name into it. Then he said, "Yes, Asa," to Corporal Purvis.

"It's about this Miss Collins, sir. Seems like she's smashed up her car pretty bad, Inspector. Knocked over on its side, her Volks is. Down below the Flats, the car is. I'm calling from the Three Oaks, sir. Miss Collins is——"

"Is she hurt? How badly hurt?" Heimrich's voice was abrupt, demanding.

"She says not, sir. Says she isn't hurt at all. Just shaken up a little. Bruised some, maybe. She was standing by the car when I got there, you see. Had got out of it, somehow. Was just standing there, looking at it."

"She's with you now? At Armstrong's saloon?"

"She's out in my car, sir. Wanted to know if there's any place around here she can rent a car. She says she's got to drive on to New York."

"Tell her there isn't," Heimrich said. "And drive her to Dr. Chandler for a checkup. I'll call the doctor and set it up. If he says she's all right, take her back to the inn. What does she say happened? Hit an icy stretch and skidded off the road?"

"No, sir. What she says happened, a station wagon cut in front of her and forced her off. That's what she says, Inspector. A little farther on there's that ditch, sir. If she'd tipped into that—well, it wouldn't have been so good."

Another station wagon? Or the same station wagon? Why hadn't the girl listened to Susan? Why hadn't he—

"All right, Asa. Get her to the doctor's for a going over. Get your father to pick up the Volks. Take her back to the inn, if Dr. Chandler says she's up to it. Stay there yourself. Lieutenant Forniss and I'll be over in a few minutes. Right?"

Purvis said "Sir" and hung up. I should have made it an order, Heimrich thought. I should have made it material witness. If Michael's girl isn't all right it's my fault. He called Dr. Ernest Chandler. "Doctor's office is full of people, Inspector. Of course, if it's an emergency."

"It is. Ask the doctor to call me at the inn, if she isn't all right. Or to call me anyway."

"I'll ask him to do that, Inspector."

Heimrich called his home. Susan answered after four rings. He told her what he had to tell her and she said, "Oh, damn! I tried to get her not to. Tried hard. But she wouldn't listen. The sweet, crazy kid."

"My fault," Heimrich told her. "I should have made it an order. Don't leave Van Brunt. Young Purvis is taking her back to the inn if she's up to it. You might——"

"Of course, dear. I'll have to fill the oil stove, and then I'll go right down. You think she was forced off the road? By a—a station wagon?"

"What Asa says she told him. Be sure the stove's off before you try to fill it."

"Yes, dear," Susan Heimrich said. "I always do, Merton." And she hung up.

"An accident," Heimrich told Alice Arnold. "We may have to come back later. There may be one or two things more we'll need to ask you."

She said, "Of course, Inspector. I guess I'll have to stay here for a while, anyway. People will be calling, I suppose."

"Probably," Heimrich said. "Well—" He moved to join Forniss, already at the door from the office.

"There's one thing," Miss Arnold said. "I don't suppose it means anything. But you did ask me if there was anything new in Mr. Jackson's practice. Recently had been, and I said there hadn't. Because it slipped my mind. I'm not really tracking very well today, I'm afraid."

"You're doing fine," Heimrich told her. "You have thought of something?"

"Only," she said, "that Mr. Jackson is defending that Mrs. Kemper. The one they say killed Mr. Lord. Up in Cold Harbor. Last Fourth of July. I suppose you'd have to call that a criminal practice, Inspector. I should have thought of it right away. Only when you asked about criminal practices, somehow I thought of gangsters. People like that. Not people like poor Mrs. Kemper, although everybody says she did do it. Shot him while he was making a speech, you know."

Heimrich did know, although his knowledge was not at first hand. On the Fourth of July, he and Susan had been in Italy on holiday. Probably when Burton Lord, retired or semiretired producer, had been shot to death while making a speech at his third annual Fourth of July picnic, Heimrich and Susan had been having an after-dinner drink on the terrace outside the bar of the Gritti Palace, watching boats on the Grand Canal.

Heimrich had not known that Sam Jackson had been counsel for Loren Kemper, twenty-odd-year-old widow of Anthony Kemper— and allegedly mistress of Burton Lord—indicted by the Putnam County grand jury on a charge of murder in the first degree and in jail at the county seat of Carmel, N.Y. The information surprised him somewhat. Jackson had not, as far as Heimrich knew, been a trial lawyer. Oh, a few times in civil cases. Heimrich remembered that once, several years ago, Sam had represented the plaintiff in an automobile accident suit—and won it, too, although up against insurance company lawyers.

Heimrich thanked Alice Arnold for her belated recollection. He and Forniss walked the long dark corridor to the outer office and down the stairs into the winter sunshine. The wind was still blustery and cold as they crossed Van Brunt Avenue toward the inn. But ice had melted off the pavement and the sun had almost dried it.

"See any way his defense of Mrs. Kemper could tie in, Charlie?" Heimrich asked as they crossed the also-drying parking lot.

"Nope," Forniss said. "Nor why Jackson got mixed up in it. From all I hear, it's open and shut. Shut for the Kemper babe, which is what she is, they tell me. Oh, try to get an all-male jury, which just might decide she's too pretty to be locked up for the rest of her life. Lot of people saw her with the rifle, they told me, including District Attorney Peters himself. He happened to be one of the guests. Swore himself in before the grand jury and testified he saw her shoot. Used a rifle. Had to, since she was maybe a hundred yards away. Pretty good shooting at that. Only she's—she was, I ought to say—a member of some rifle club and pretty good. Why Jackson took the case God knows. Open and shut, like I said."

He said that as they went into the taproom. The fire had been built up; Joe was behind his bar, polishing glasses, although the bar did not open until noon. Still, the day before Christmas. People tend to get thirsty early on the day before Christmas.

Michael Faye was sitting at a table near the fireplace and drinking coffee. He, to his stepfather, looked forlorn.

"Joan's gone on to New York," Michael said, and sounded forlorn. "Mother tried to argue her out of it, and I tried, God knows. But she wouldn't listen. Kept saying she'd promised her father. Thing is, I don't think she even likes him very much. Her father, I mean. She's a crazy kid, Dad. Gets ideas in her head and—"

He ended it with a shrug.

Then he said, "Ready to take me home, Dad? Maybe we could still pick up a tree. Only, hell, there can't be any lights, can there? Or weren't you and Mother going to have a tree?"

"We'll pick up a tree," Merton Heimrich told the boy, at the moment so much a boy, and so disconsolate. "Only not quite yet, Michael. You see, something's come—"

He stopped, because he heard a car stop outside. He looked at the door to the parking lot. So did Michael and Lieutenant Forniss.

It was Corporal Purvis who pulled open the door. Then he stood aside, and Joan Collins came into the room. She walked steadily. She walked to the fire and reached her hands out toward it. Then she said, "I'm all right, Michael dear. Perfectly all right." But there was, Heimrich thought, strain in the young voice.

Michael looked at her. Then he got up and went to her. He said her name and, "So you changed your mind. That's wonderful."

She merely looked at him for a moment. Then she held her hands out toward him.

"You could call it that," Joan said, and managed a rather stiff smile. "You sound as if you didn't——"

"I was just about to tell him, Joan," Heimrich said. "She—well, she had her mind changed for her, Michael. You're all right, my dear? You're sure you're all right?"

"Not a scratch," Joan said. "You can ask the doctor. There's a bruise on my right arm and the doctor says it will probably turn black and blue. I banged into something, I guess. But not hard enough to matter, really. The doctor says it was a good thing I was wearing a safety belt. But I always do, of course. What about the car, Inspector?"

Heimrich looked at Asa Purvis.

"Dad's going to check it out, sir," Purvis said. "He'll call you and let you know. I asked him not to do anything about it until you'd had a chance to look at it, Inspector. I—I guess I told him that was what you said, sir. Because——"

"Yes, Corporal," Heimrich said. "You were quite right. We do want to have a look at Miss Collins's car."

Michael was looking at his girl. There was bewilderment in his eyes and on his face. Then he looked at Heimrich.

"Joan had an accident, son," Heimrich said. "Down the road a bit. Hit an icy patch and——"

"No," Joan Collins said. "It wasn't the ice. Didn't Corporal—it's Purvis, isn't it?—didn't he tell you? I was forced off the road. By a driver who—well, who was half-witted or something. Somebody in a big station wagon. He cut—"

After Forniss and the Inspector had gone to see Sam Jackson's secretary; after Susan Heimrich and Michael had tried, without success, to dissuade her from going on to New York—"Dad was expecting me. I knew he'd start climbing walls"—Michael had driven them back to the house above the Hudson. He had carried her cases down and stowed them in the Buick. He had insisted on driving, because there could still be icy spots.

(He is an all-right driver, Heimrich thought. Susan's a better one. But children usually think of their parents as tottering.)

They had had no trouble getting to the house, or in stowing the suitcases in the red Volks; no trouble in starting the Volks. Michael had ridden with Joan, Susan following in the Buick after she had checked the fire. And "Done a few things around the house." Apparently she was still doing them.

"I dropped Michael off here," Joan said. "He told me which way to go. Down the state road to thirty-five, and then on the Taconic. I knew the way from there."

She had driven on N.Y. 11-F for a few miles, along a straight stretch "with little houses close together on both sides of the road, some of them rather rundown. Not like the rest of the houses around here. Michael says there's something you call it."

"She means the Flats, Dad," Michael said. Parents are not only tottering. They have a tendency to be dim-witted. Heimrich said, "Yes, Michael." He refrained from adding, "Thank you," although that took a little effort. "Then, Joan?"

She had been perhaps two miles beyond the last of the small houses of the area which almost constitutes a country slum, when she saw, in the mirror, a car overtaking her. "It seemed to be coming on awfully fast. There were still icy spots down there. I was going very slowly, because I didn't want to skid on the ice."

The following car was a big station wagon. It passed the little red Volks—"It must have been going at least sixty"—and immediately cut in ahead. "He was so close he scraped my fender turning in in front of me. And he didn't have to, Inspector. There wasn't anything coming the other way. It was—it was as if he meant to. Like those crazy drivers in TV series, you know. The cars always turn over. Usually they catch fire. They look like brand-new cars, most of the time."

"Yes," Heimrich said, "they do waste a lot of cars. You kept yours on the road?"

"Not really. He didn't leave me any road to keep on. I fought Jenny—that's what I call her, Inspector. But I—I guess I must have been on the shoulder. Anyway, she tipped over. Not all the way over. Leaned over's more like it. Against a bank, really. And there was a lot of noise—scraping and breaking noises. And I was half-way across the seat, but the belt stopped me. I banged my arm against something, I guess. I didn't really notice. I was fighting Jenny. Still trying to hold her on the road. Then I pushed the door up and managed to get out. I was—oh, just standing and looking at Jenny when the Corporal came along and stopped. Maybe I was shaking a little, I guess."

"You had reason to be," Heimrich told her. "You see this accident, Corporal?"

"I saw Miss Collins's car ahead going through the Flats, sir. I was maybe a couple of miles behind her. The station wagon passed me, too. She's right, sir. It was going at excessive speed. For the road conditions. Maybe I should have chased him down, Inspector. But I was on my way to the Reverend Armstrong's, Inspector. To ask about his wagon like you said to do, sir."

"All right, Asa. You were too far back to see the accident. Happen to get the number of this wagon that was going too fast for road conditions?"

"I should have, but I guess I didn't, Inspector. I did look but the plate seemed to have mud smeared on it. There's a lot of mud around, sir. Now it's begun to thaw a little some places. Anyhow, like I said, I'd decided to let him get away with it."

"Miss Collins, I suppose you didn't get the license number of this wagon that cut in front of you?"

"No. I was fighting Jenny. It was just a big station wagon. Painted a dark color, I think. Dark blue, maybe. Or just a very dark gray."

"Like the one you saw in the parking lot last night?"

"Pretty much, I guess. But I couldn't say it was the same one,

Inspector. It all happened so fast. And I—I guess I was too scared to notice much of anything. And too busy trying to keep my car on the road. I—I think I kept seeing all those cars turning over on TV and—and exploding."

Suddenly she seemed to sway. Michael had an arm around her shoulders. He put her in a chair. He kept his arm around her. Michael looked hard at his stepfather. His gaze was not actually inimical. It was not especially friendly, either.

"One more question, Joan," Heimrich said. "Was there ice on the road where this happened? Ice the wagon might have skidded on? Skidded in front of you?"

She hadn't noticed any; not just there.

"And after he brushed you, the driver didn't stop. And do you know whether the driver was a man or a woman?"

It was more than one question, and this time Michael shook his head.

The station wagon had gone on. It had not even slowed. If anything, it had gone on faster. Joan hadn't noticed the sex of the driver. She had merely been trying to keep her little car on the road—and seeing cars burst into flame on TV screens. There was still one more question, and Heimrich started it.

"Do you know anyone," he said, and the door from the parking lot opened again. It was Susan Heimrich who came in this time. She stopped just inside the door and started to speak. She said, "That half-witted dog of ours—" But then she saw Joan Collins, sitting in a straight chair with Michael's arm protectingly about her.

It had to be told all over again. When she had been told, Susan went to Joan Collins and crouched in front of her and looked, very carefully, into the girl's face.

"Yes," Joan said, "I'm really all right, Mrs. Heimrich. Didn't get hurt. Just shaken up a little is all."

Susan continued to look at her for a moment. Then she turned and looked at her husband.

"Yes, dear," Merton said, answering a question which had not been asked, "Dr. Chandler's seen her. Can't find anything wrong. That's what she tells us, anyway."

"You've talked to Ernest, Merton? Checked with him?"

Heimrich admitted he had not talked to Dr. Ernest Chandler. Susan shook her head, and her eyes said a pejorative "*Men!*" and she left them for the office and, Heimrich knew, the telephone. He also knew that it wouldn't make much difference if "Doctor's with a patient, Mrs. Heimrich." Ernest Chandler would talk to Susan Heimrich.

"What I was about to ask, Joan," Heimrich said. "Does anybody here in the village know you by sight? Anybody you know of?"

"No," Joan said. "You mean, how did somebody last night know I was the one at the window? The one who might know—well, who was driving the wagon that killed Mr. Jackson. That's what you're wondering, isn't it?"

"Yes, my dear, that's what I'm wondering. And knew you were driving a red Volks."

"No," she said again, "I don't know of anyone here who would recognize me. And try to kill me because I might have seen too much from the window. That's also what you mean, isn't it, Inspector?"

"One of the things I'm wondering about, yes."

"You do think it was the same station wagon both times? And that the idea was to kill me so I couldn't talk? But I have talked. Told you everything I know."

"Whoever killed Jackson may not know that," Heimrich said. "May not, anyway, be sure of that. Not want to take a chance on that. Yes, Joan. There's a chance somebody wants to keep you from talking. On a witness stand, perhaps. Where it wouldn't be hearsay. What I say you said, if you know what I mean."

She nodded her head, the waist-long hair flowing around it. She pushed the long hair back. Then she said, "I could sign a statement, couldn't I? A statement about what I saw? So then it wouldn't matter so much whether I'm alive or not. Except to me, of course. Oh, all right, Michael."

The last, Heimrich thought, was response to the tightening of Michael Faye's arm, which still held her close.

"A lot of people know me, Dad," Michael said. "And know I'm your son, of course. And anybody could have seen Joan and me together. Seen us all together last night when we got here. Maybe someone already sitting in this station wagon. Maybe already waiting for Mr. Jackson to come out. And seen Mother and Joan and me together this morning when we were getting into the car to drive home. And followed us. And seen Joan drop me off here and drive away in Jenny. Jenny's—well, Jenny's pretty obvious, Dad."

"Yes, son," Heimrich said. "It could have been that way."

There was no point in telling Michael that his tottering stepfather had already thought it could have been that way, or that a light going on in an upstairs window a few minutes after the Heimrichs and their son and—their future daughter-in-law—entered the inn would give somebody material to guess on. Particularly when a light went on again in the same window at a time most inopportune for a murderer. A light in a window and a curtain drawn back so someone could look out.

"You did say you pulled back the curtain when you saw Mr. Jackson last night, didn't you, Joan?" he said.

Michael and Joan both looked at him, with the expressions of those slightly puzzled by an irrelevancy.

"Why, I guess so," Joan said. "I must have. I wanted to see if it was still raining. Be sure it wouldn't rain in after I opened the window."

Chapter 7

AN APB WENT OUT. Subject: Large station wagon, dark blue or, perhaps, dark gray; possibly brought into a garage or body shop for rear-end repairs to right rear fender, which might be dented; probably not now wearing chains; chains possibly still in the wagon.

"They won't be," Forniss said. "In a garage somewhere, washed nice and clean. And backing into a man isn't like backing into a stone wall. Men—well, men are softer. Don't dent a car so much."

Heimrich gave an agreeing "Mmm." They were driving north on N.Y. 11-F. They were driving toward Cold Harbor and the residence of the late Burton Lord and the present Amelia Lord. Forniss knew the way. He had been at the Lord house, at what remained of a picnic, on the last Fourth of July. He had been there on duty. He had not performed much duty.

"The D.A. took over," Forniss told Heimrich as they pulled out of the inn's lot and out onto an almost dry Van Brunt Avenue. The sun was melting ice from trees; trees were dripping. Only in a few shaded spots did ice still cling to the pavements. Near The Corners a tree had come down, and taken wires with it. A crew from the Dunlop Tree Service was sawing the tree up; a crew from the New York State Gas and Electric Company was clinging to poles, and yelling back and forth. But it might be a crew from Connecticut or

New Jersey, called in to lend a hand. At least, somebody was trying.

They pulled in at Purvis's Garage. Jenny, the red Volks, was standing in front of the garage, out of the way of anybody who might want to buy gas. Jenny looked considerably banged up. The right side was bashed.

One of the many Purvis boys—Obadiah, Heimrich guessed—came out of the office to help them look at the little red car. "Lot of body work, it'll need," he told them. "Have to take it to the body shop up at the Harbor. I'd guess. Maybe cost more than the car's worth."

Heimrich agreed that Jenny would need a lot of body work.

"Only," the Purvis boy said, "engine seems to be O.K. And the frame ain't damaged much, far as we can tell. So maybe."

Heimrich said "Mmm" and looked at the left front fender of the Volks. It was scraped and rather deeply dented. It would need rolling out and repainting. It might even need to be replaced. The car had tipped on its right side into the bank when it went off N.Y. 11-F. The station wagon which had sideswiped Jenny would show similar marks of scraping. Probably on the right rear fender. Probably with red paint ground in. Heimrich used the office telephone to add to the things to be looked for on a large, dark-colored station wagon, make unknown.

They went back to the police car and on north toward Cold Harbor and the Lords' house. Forniss drove.

"It's not much to go on, is it?" Forniss said. "Sam Jackson was defending this Mrs. Kemper. So? She's going to need somebody. Need somebody damn bad. With the D.A. himself a witness against her. Actually saw her fire the gun. Swore himself in before the grand jury and testified, you know. And he was not the only one saw her, M.L. Open and shut, like I said."

Heimrich said it did sound like it. And he agreed that they did not have much to go on. "Only," he said, "it was a break in pattern. Sam Jackson's pattern. He didn't handle criminal cases. Then all at once he takes one on. A pretty hopeless one. And then he gets killed. Probably no connection, I'll admit. But—two breaks in a man's pattern, Charlie. Doing something unusual for him and getting killed. Sort of thing we look for, wouldn't you say, Charlie? And about all we've got until we find this damn wagon."

Forniss said, "Yeah." He did not say it with enthusiasm. Then he said, "Hey, the traffic light's on."

It was the first of Cold Harbor's three traffic lights. It was on, all right. It was on red. Forniss stopped for it. "Wonder about on up," Forniss said, and used the radio. Yes, power was on again at the barracks. And one station wagon had showed up for repairs, at a garage in Poughkeepsie. But it was a light green station wagon and it had skidded into a tree. People in another car had seen it skid into the tree. It had also raised hell with the tree. Sure, they had the owner's name and address. A local doctor. If the Lieutenant wanted the name? Forniss didn't.

"They're really working on this one," Forniss said, and pulled ahead as the light turned green. "The electric company guys, I mean. Last time it took them damn near a week, some places."

The next light turned green just as they reached it. A filling station had a light on over a sign which read "ICE COLD BEER." And on the business block of Main Street, which 11-F became for half a dozen blocks, shops were lighted. On the sidewalk in front of Herzog's Hardware, a young couple was looking for the right Christmas tree in a stack of trees. A clerk was helping them look. The best trees would be gone by now, Heimrich thought. They would be set up in houses, and people would be putting ornaments on them, and stringing lights through them. Would Michael be able to find a decent tree anywhere? And will I be home on Christmas Eve to look at it? And will the repair crews have worked down to Van Brunt by this evening?

They had to wait at the traffic light. Then they were out of Cold Harbor. The yellow warning was blinking at the shopping center. Things were getting back to normal. Except that Sam Jackson was dead. When Heimrich had driven past the shopping center the evening before, Sam had been alive and, presumably, expecting to remain so.

A mile or so beyond the shopping center, Forniss guided the car left onto a narrow blacktop. A just discernible sign read "HAWTHORNE DRIVE." A more visible sign said "DEAD END." "Last place on it's the Lords',", Forniss said, and followed the road's sharp turn to the right and stopped the car. It skidded a little as he put the brakes on. Tall trees shaded the road there. And a branch from one of them lay halfway across the pavement. The Dunlop Tree Service hadn't yet got round to side roads.

"Guess we can make it," Forniss said, and proved they could—just could, with twigs scratching the right side of the police car.

"Pull up for a minute, Charlie," Heimrich said, with the fallen limb safely behind them. "Fill me in a bit before we see Mrs. Lord to check up on what she's going to say at the trial. As District Attorney Peters has asked us to."

Forniss pulled the car to the side of the road and stopped it there. He did not go off on the softened shoulder. If some other car wanted to pass it would have to wait its turn.

"Thing is," Forniss said, "it was pretty much wrapped up by the time I got there. Like I said, M.L., Peters is pretty much a takeover guy. He'd got a couple of county detectives down before it got to us. Got to us roundabout. Nothing much left for us by the time the Sergeant and I got there. Jenkins and I could just as well have stood in bed. And it was hot as hell."

It is likely to be hot in the late afternoon of the Fourth of July. Forniss and Sergeant Jenkins had got to the Lords' picnic at a little before six. There wasn't, by then, much picnic left to get to. Burton Lord had been dead since around four thirty. "As nearly as they could pin it down." Most of the hundred or so guests at Burton Lord's third annual, and last, picnic had been allowed to go home.

"Peters himself had taken off, M.L. Left a county detective named Jones over at the Kemper house to keep an eye on Mrs. Kemper. I talked to Detective Connolly, who'd set a little table up and was asking people what they'd seen. Most of them hadn't seen so damn much. Or, I guess, heard too damn much of what Lord was saying. Most of them were sitting around in the shade with their drinks and Lord was up on this sort of platform spouting. One man said Lord was pretty funny when he started, but that he'd sort of wound down. Said it had been the same way at the other two picnics, and that maybe people didn't listen too hard toward the end. Lord was still going strong at around four twenty-five, maybe four thirty, when he stopped. Stopped because he was dead."

Lord had, Forniss had been told, been shot by a slim woman with long blond hair, from the Kemper property. She had used a rifle; she had been about a hundred yards—perhaps 150—from her target. "Show you about where when we get there, M.L."

"Pretty good shooting," Heimrich said.

"Yeah. Only it seems this Mrs. Kemper is—I guess it's 'was' now —a member of a rifle team. Country club rifle team. Was a damn good shot. Everybody agrees to that. She doesn't deny that herself. Does deny having fired at Lord. Says she was at the swimming pool on the other side of the house. Trouble is, people saw her fire. Not a lot of people, Connolly told me. Maybe half a dozen. But one of them was the honorable Jonathan Peters, district attorney of Putnam County. They'll all swear it was Loren Kemper, all right. Four of them did for the grand jury, including Mr. Takeover himself."

"Only four of this half dozen, Charlie?"

"All Peters called. Probably figured four was enough. Seems to have been. He got a true bill in less than half an hour, from what I hear. They all said the same thing, according to the minutes. Loren Kemper just stood up in plain sight on this slope—show you when we get there—and took aim and fired. The slug got Lord in the back of the head. Right where she meant it to. Like you said, pretty good shooting."

"Perfect shooting," Heimrich said. "After she'd killed him, Charlie? What did she do then?"

"According to Connolly, who says he got it from the D.A., she leaned down and rubbed the rifle in the grass. Getting prints off, probably. And then took off for her house at a dead run. Went into it. Was still there when the county boys went over. Didn't know what they were talking about. Hadn't heard a shot. Yeah, she owned a rifle. Right in the hall closet, where it always was. Handy near the front door if she needed it. Had kept it there for years. Only, M.L., they looked in the closet and it wasn't there. It was out in the grass where she'd used it. She didn't deny it was her gun. Had no idea how it got there. She'd just come in from the pool and changed into slacks and a yellow sports shirt when the county boys got there. She could show them her wet swim suit. It was hanging up to dry in one of the bathrooms."

"Was it, Charlie?"

"Yep. Just as she said."

"What was she wearing when she shot Lord? Was seen shooting him?"

"Dark slacks and a yellow shirt, same as she had on when Connolly and Jones got there. Yellow blouse and dark slacks—dark blue, as it turned out. This is all what I got told, M.L. They'd taken her over to Carmel by the time Jenkins and I got there. Held her overnight, seeing it was a holiday. Charged her as a material witness. She had a lawyer by that time. Not Jackson. Somebody from Brewster. Judge set bail at fifty thousand. She'd put it up and was back home that afternoon. On the fifth, that is."

"Only material witness, Charlie? Why not suspicion of homicide, and without bail pending action by the grand jury?"

Forniss didn't know. Heimrich would have to ask District Attorney Peters about that.

"Yes," Heimrich said. "We'll have to ask Mr. Peters about that. We'd better go along and see Mrs. Lord, Charlie. Go over the testimony she's going to give at the trial. The way Mr. Peters told us to."

Forniss looked at Heimrich for a long moment before he said, "Did he, M.L.?"

"Way I remember it," Heimrich said.

Forniss drove them on along the narrow road. They passed a driveway with a wooden sign at the foot of it. The sign read: "KEMPER." A few hundred yards beyond that there was another driveway. This time the sign was of metal, and rather larger. It read: "THE LORDS." Forniss turned into the drive.

"By the way, Charlie," Heimrich said, "happen to know whether Sam Jackson was at this picnic?"

Forniss didn't know. It might be the District Attorney's boys had made a list, but he rather doubted it.

Heimrich doubted it too. There's little point in beating the bushes when the quarry is in plain sight. Stupidly in plain sight of a hundred or so picnickers, even if most of them were not looking.

No tree limbs lay across the hard-surfaced drive to the Lord house. The driveway twisted itself around a big maple tree, which had lost only twigs and which dripped on them as they passed it. The house was large and white and of no particular style. It did have two tall white pillars in front of it. They supported a porch roof. Doors of a two- or three-car garage near the house were closed. There was no sign of life in the house as Forniss parked the police car on the turnaround, headed out.

"Over there the picnic was," Forniss said, and pointed. What he pointed to was a lawn area of perhaps two acres—more than an acre certainly. It was a level stretch; the grass, now under slowly melting ice, had been close-mowed. A big oak tree, last summer's browned leaves clinging tenaciously to it, was near the center of the roughly rectangular area. A large maple grew at one end of the close-mowed area—the end nearest the narrow, dead-ending Hawthorne Drive; hence at the westerly end of the picnic ground. Both trees would have provided shade to sit in on a hot July afternoon.

Beyond the grassy rectangle was a line of bushes—barbed bushes, Heimrich supposed, making what their purveyors call a living fence. Beyond them, the land rose rather steeply and at the top of the rise was another big white house. There were evergreens in front of this house, partly sheltering it—giving it a hint of privacy.

"Kemper property beyond the bushes," Forniss said. "Way I got it, she stood about halfway up the slope to do her shooting. Lord seems to have been on a little platform facing this way while he made his Fourth of July speech. Oration, maybe you'd call it. Mostly little jokes about his guests, somebody told me. Not the grand old flag sort of speech. Sort of folksy, way I got it. With a lot of theater reminiscences thrown in. He'd been a Broadway producer, you know. Still produced now and then. Not so many hits, they say. But he made a pile while the going was good, I guess. Anyway, this setup looks like he'd made a pile some time."

"He did musicals mostly," Heimrich said. "If I'm thinking of the right Lord. A few straight plays. One of them ran almost as long as *Life with Father*. Four, five years ago that would have been. Probably made everybody concerned quite a bit of money. Let's see if Mrs. Lord's at home, Charlie."

The doorbell of the big house was answered promptly. It was answered by an elderly man in a black jacket and, rather surprisingly, striped trousers. He thought Mrs. Lord probably was at home. He would ascertain. And who should he say—?

Heimrich told him who he should say, and that he and Lieutenant Forniss were there at the request of District Attorney Peters. And that they would, he hoped, not need to keep Mrs. Lord long. The man said, "Thank you, Inspector. You can wait inside, if you like. Although Mrs. Lord may still be at breakfast."

It was almost eleven thirty by the watch on Heimrich's wrist. But Mrs. Lord's breakfast hours were no concern of his. They went into a big foyer. It was pleasantly warm in the large room, which had wide, closed doors on either side of it and a wide staircase mounting out of it. The butler, imported by the sound of his speech, opened the door on the right and went through it and closed it after him. It was very still in the foyer. The noise of the wind, which was whipping outside, did not penetrate. There was a rather ornate lamp on the table near the foot of the staircase. It was lighted. Power on here, apparently. Unless the house had its own generator, which it might well have.

The man in the black jacket came back into the room. If the gentlemen would please come this way? He held the wide door open.

Mrs. Amelia Lord was sitting in her living room—drawing room? —in front of a fire. She was drinking coffee and smoking a cigarette. She did not look as if she should be called "Amelia." Merton Heimrich felt sympathy, from one misnamed to another.

She was a slim woman in a black dress. She had red-gold hair, very recently styled by someone very good—someone, at a guess, in New York City. Her jawline was firm, untarnished. She might, he thought, be in her fifties. But she had almost pushed ten of those years away.

Heimrich said he hoped they weren't intruding and that Mr.

Peters had asked them to have a word with her. To be sure everything was clear in her mind before——

"Before that awful woman goes on trial," Amelia Lord said. "I suppose that's what you mean. About that day. Why does he think it isn't all clear in my mind? Horribly clear. It will always be. *Always*. How could anybody think it wouldn't be? Clear—and hideous?"

"I'm sure it is," Heimrich said. "And I'm sorry—well, to have to bring it up again. But, in his position, Mr. Peters has to be very sure about everybody's testimony. It's—well, just a matter of routine."

She didn't see what doubt there could be, what could possibly need clarification. "People saw her—saw that bitch—kill Burton," she said. "Who was her lover. Who broke it off. Jonathan Peters saw it himself. Saw her fire the shot and then run up to her house. What more does anybody need?"

"I don't know, Mrs. Lord," Heimrich said. "Thing is, a district attorney prosecuting a murder case has to be sure—as sure as he can be—that the defense doesn't come up with something unexpected, some surprise. Did you, personally, see Mrs. Kemper fire the shot, Mrs. Lord?"

"Plenty of people did," she said. "All he'll need, surely." Her voice was soft, modulated. But each word was clear, sharply enunciated. Her voice had not risen, not become strident, even when she called Loren Kemper a bitch. She's entirely in control, Heimrich thought. Of her mind, of her body, even of her voice. As a well-trained actor needs to be. Had she been an actress, Heimrich wondered? Had she schooled her body and her voice? Appeared, perhaps, in some of her husband's plays? It wasn't, of course, important.

"You yourself, Mrs. Lord. Did you see Mrs. Kemper shoot your husband?"

She didn't see what difference it made, since so many had. But no, she hadn't actually seen the shot fired. She had had to go into the house. "To see about some things." Heimrich waited, a little noticeably.

"It wasn't anything really important," Amelia Lord said. "But I was the hostess, after all. Most people brought their own food, of course. Some brought enough for a dozen people. And the men Mr. Lord had up from the city—to tend bar and that sort of thing— did almost all there was to be done. Still, I had to keep an eye on things. You can see that, can't you, Inspector?"

She sounded, Heimrich thought, a little defensive. Because she had walked out on her husband's speech—his last speech—to see about some things? Possibly.

"We were running out of ice," she said. "The men we'd hired brought some with them, of course. But it was a hot day, a terribly hot day, and almost everybody was having long drinks. We provided the drinks, of course. Alan had gone in to get some more ice, out of those bag machines, you know, but it was taking him longer than I'd thought it would. So I went to check. He might have come back without my seeing him, you see. And it really seemed— well, almost an emergency. A trivial thing like that, on that terrible, dreadful day."

Her beautifully controlled voice faltered just perceptibly. She said, "I'm sorry, Inspector. It—things keep coming back. Awful things."

"Of course, Mrs. Lord. And I'm sorry I have to bring them back. But one of the things Mr. Peters found he wasn't entirely clear about was why you had gone into the house while your husband was still speaking. One of the things he wanted me to clear up. You have cleared it up, of course. Had Alan come back with the ice, Mrs. Lord? Not that it matters, naturally."

"No. He'd had to go way beyond Cold Harbor before he found a machine with ice in it. The one in the shopping center was empty. It was such a hot day, you know. He had to go clear through town to the Gulf station on the other side, and the traffic was bad. And even there, he got the last two bags. By the time he got back, well, people were beginning to leave, you know. Because Burton was—dead." She looked into the lively fire for some seconds. Then she said "Dead" again. And her voice was dead.

Once more, Heimrich said he was sorry, that he realized how hard this must be for her. She merely nodded her head to show that she had heard him. Then she lighted a fresh cigarette from the stub of the old. She ground out the butt of the finished cigarette, very slowly and very carefully.

"There's just one thing," Heimrich said. "Probably Mr. Peters knows already and anyway it doesn't matter. Who is Alan, Mrs. Lord? The man who let us in?"

"No. The butler's named Carson. Alan is my son, Inspector. Alan Lord. Legally Lord. Burton adopted him after we were married. I'd divorced his real father. George Nolan, his father was. Is, actually. He's still writing that column of his. Attacking people still, I suppose. Of course, I never read it now. Or see him. It must be six or seven years since I've laid eyes on George."

Heimrich ran the name through his memory. At first, nothing came of this. George Nolan? Nothing. Then a glimmer of something. A syndicated newspaper columnist? The *Times*? No. The *Times* had only its own columnists. It didn't syndicate them. *The Daily News*, then? It didn't feel right. The Nolan stirring faintly in his memory was a liberal—what conservatives, for no apparent reason, referred to as a "so-called liberal." Therefore not, most obviously not, *The New York Daily News*. Which left the *Post* and the big Long Island paper. Heimrich seldom saw the *Post*, never the paper published on Long Island. Somebody had mentioned Nolan to Heimrich, or in Heimrich's hearing. Mentioned him favorably, it felt like. Sam Jackson? It was possible; it was even probable. Jackson had been one of the few liberals, so-called or otherwise, in Van Brunt. He had even been a Democrat, which was almost unheard of.

The mind wanders, in search of wraiths. He brought it back.

"By the way, Mrs. Lord, was a Mr. Jackson one of the guests at the picnic?" Heimrich asked, and stood up.

She said, "Jackson?"

"Samuel Jackson. A lawyer in Van Brunt."

"I'm afraid I don't really know, Inspector. It was Burton who invited people—most of them, anyway. Most of them from New York. People we'd known in the theater. Some locals, of course. Neighbors we'd met since we'd moved here. Five years ago, that was. And had it done over, of course. It's an old house, you know.

Inside it was—well, drab. Little squinchy windows. Burton had three rooms put together to make this one."

His was not the only mind to go its own wayward course, Merton Heimrich thought. He looked around the big room—forty feet by twenty, at a guess. And with a picture window making up a good part of one wall. A window which overlooked the picnic ground, and gave a good view of the Kemper house on its not-too-distant hill. Not the kind of room native to old Hudson Valley houses. A somewhat stagey room? Mind wandering again? Apparently.

Amelia Lord, facing the fire, had her back to the window.

"Samuel Jackson," she said, speaking to the fire. "Haven't I heard—Oh! Isn't a lawyer named Jackson defending the woman, the awful woman, who killed Burton?" She looked at Heimrich then.

"Yes, Mrs. Lord. Sam Jackson was Mrs. Kemper's lawyer."

"Why would he do that? Why would anyone? Everybody knows she's guilty. *Everybody.* He must be—oh, some kind of shyster. Burton would never invite a man like that here."

"Sam Jackson wasn't a shyster," Heimrich told her. "He was a very highly respected lawyer. His family has been in these parts for generations. And we may never know why he took Mrs. Kemper's case. We can't ask him because, you see, he was killed last night. In an automobile accident. You don't remember his having been at the picnic on the Fourth of July?"

She shook her head.

"No. What did he look like, Inspector? He could have been here, I suppose. There were so many people. I didn't really know them all. People Burton knew from way back. Some of them I merely knew by name—by reputation. Actors, directors, set designers, some of them before my time. And, I suppose, people he'd just met recently and invited—oh, on the spur of the moment. He liked big parties, you know. And he loved this place of ours, and loved people to come and see it. And, of course, he did know so many people. And when he invited people, they were always glad to come. After all, he was Burton Lord."

"And a very celebrated man," Heimrich said, adding what she had not quite said.

"A wonderful man," she told him. "A genius, really."

Heimrich had not quite expected that, but he nodded his head, indicating accord. He said that that would be all they needed to trouble her about, and that they were sorry they had had to trouble her at all; to make her think about the past.

"Yes," she said, and stubbed out her cigarette and stood up. She moved fluently. "I am trying to forget that awful day," she said. "I even invited some friends here for dinner last night. The first time since last summer I've felt—well, up to seeing anybody. And then, that storm. I'd only asked twelve—just a very little dinner party, really. And four of them couldn't get here because of the ice. And the electricity was out all around here, Carson tells me. I hadn't realized it was that bad."

It seemed to Heimrich that, although she had not much wanted to see them, she now was loath to have them go. A woman lonely in a too big house, he thought. (A big house with, obviously, its own electric generator.) He said that it had been a bad night, but that the ice was thawing now. He said, "Your son isn't around, Mrs. Lord?"

"No, he's off somewhere with friends. You didn't want to see him, did you, Inspector? As I told you, he wasn't even here when his father was killed."

"No, there's nothing we need to see your son about. Nothing he could add, obviously. I—oh, I was just afraid we'd upset you. Might want somebody around. No, we've nothing to ask your son, Mrs. Lord. The District Attorney just wanted us to talk to you. To make sure he had everything straight. Had the whole picture. We have it now. And I'm sorry we had to bother you about it."

It was all right, she told him. And she did understand Mr. Peters had to make sure about everything, with the trial so close. The second of January it was to start, wasn't it?

That was the schedule, Heimrich told her. The death of Mr. Jackson might make a postponement necessary. The new defense lawyer, whoever she got, would almost certainly ask for one.

"I don't see how she'll be able to get anyone," Mrs. Lord said. "I really don't. People *saw* her fire the rifle. I don't see how she got this Jackson man, if he's as reputable as you say he is."

But her voice remained modulated. And Carson would show them out.

Carson did. He thanked them for the privilege.

Chapter 8

In the car, Forniss said, "Where now?" and Heimrich looked at his watch. It was a few minutes after noon. He said they might as well go back to the Old Stone Inn. Perhaps young Purvis had come across a station wagon. Or perhaps somebody else had, and would expect them to be at the inn.

"About time somebody found something," Forniss said. "Can't see that we did from Mrs. Lord, can you?"

Heimrich agreed that Amelia Lord hadn't helped them much. It could be they were on the wrong track entirely. But it was the only track he could see they had. "Until," he said, "we find this damn station wagon."

They went down the curving drive, around the big maple tree. They edged around the fallen branch on Hawthorne Drive. Most of the ice had gone from Hawthorne Drive. N.Y. 11-F was dry, except for a few spots in heavy shade. The sun was high and bright, but the northwest wind was cold. The night before Christmas would be a cold night, if not a white one.

The traffic lights in Cold Harbor were going about their business, which seemed to be to stop the police car. Red stopped them at each of Cold Harbor's three lights. It stopped them again in Van Brunt, at The Corners. It didn't matter too much; Heimrich couldn't see that they were going much of anywhere. Of course, things might open up. One could always hope they would.

The taproom was bright and there was a Christmas tree at one end of the bar. There were only two people in the barroom, and they were Mr. and Mrs. Clement Barkston. They looked as if they had had a good night. Elaine Barkston seemed particularly abloom. Probably she always did.

They had a table near the fire. As Heimrich and Forniss went into the room, both lifted their glasses in salute. Forniss went on to the bar; Heimrich stopped to say good morning to Barkston and his once-famous, still-beautiful wife. He said it and started on.

"Have you found out who killed the poor man, Inspector?" Elaine Barkston asked, in her soft but carrying voice.

"Not yet," Heimrich told her. "Just asking around, so far. You two making out all right?" Which was something, if not much, to say. "After missing Mrs. Lord's party. Another couple couldn't get there either. Reduced the dinner party to eight."

"Dear Amelia," Mrs. Barkston said. "Any dinner party under twenty isn't worth giving. And the poor dear's first party for months. You've been to see her, Inspector? How is dear Amelia? Such an awful thing."

"Murder is always an awful thing, Mrs. Barkston," Heimrich said.

"Most foul," she said. "As in the best it is."

The wording sounded familiar. After a second, Merton placed it. Irrelevant, of course. But what was relevant? He said, "I gather you've played Shakespeare, Mrs. Barkston?"

"When I was just a tot. A couple of centuries ago, actually. Juliet. When I was very young. And very briefly. Amelia did Lady Macbeth, once. Ten years or so ago. The only time dear Burton tried the classics. I didn't see it, but they say she was good—quite good, anyway. It didn't run long, though. Could Amelia help you any?"

"Not much, I'm afraid. A little background. I gather you two weren't at the picnic?"

"The famous picnic," Clement Barkston said. "No. We were in London then."

"At the embassy Fourth of July do," his wife said. "And a stuffy party it was. All gummed up with touring congressmen and people like that. Shouldn't we be thinking about getting along, Clem, dear? See if they'll give us lunch and be on our way home?"

Clement Barkston looked at his watch and nodded his head and said, "Maybe we'd better." He stood and held his hand down to his wife. She took the offered hand and stood. She had not used the hand for support, Heimrich thought. She had not needed to.

Heimrich joined Forniss at the bar. Forniss raised inquiring eyebrows.

"Only that Mrs. Lord used to be on the stage," Heimrich said, and reached for the martini Joe Shepley had ready for him.

They carried their drinks to a table near the fire. The inn prefers to serve lunch only in the dining room, but exceptions can be made. Joe Shepley started to come around the bar to them, but stopped and waited. Susan and Joan Collins and Michael came into the room, in that order. Susan said, "Did Asa Purvis get hold of you, Merton? He was trying to. But something seems to have happened to his radio, he says." Heimrich and Forniss stood up, and started to move toward a larger table.

"We've had lunch, Dad," Michael said. "Sort of a breakfast—lunch. We were just finishing when we saw you come in. We were about to go back to the house. The power's on again, Mrs. Cushing says."

"Yes," Heimrich said, "they've been quick, for once. Did Asa leave a message, Susan?"

"Reluctantly," Susan told him. "The boy likes to go through channels, and apparently I'm not a channel. Finally, about this station wagon."

"He's found it?"

"Well, not exactly. He's lost another. That is, Father Armstrong has."

Francis Armstrong, Doctor of Divinity and rector of St. Mary's Episcopal Church, prefers to be called Father. He is also careful to put "Roman," before "Catholic" when speaking of another persuasion.

"That's a help," Heimrich said. "Why don't we all sit down?"

They moved to a table where five could sit down. Forniss and Heimrich took their drinks with them.

"All right," Heimrich said. "Another station wagon on the loose. Tell me, dear."

"You know this candlelight service they have at St. Mary's," Susan said. "At midnight on Christmas Eve. Winding down the hill in procession, everybody carrying candles. Father Armstrong was worried about the wind. And then all back to the church for holy communion."

Heimrich knew about St. Mary's traditional service. Had never attended it. "So?"

The previous afternoon, sometime around three, Armstrong thought, he had gone from the rectory to the church. There were "things to be seen to" in connection with the candle ceremony. He was not sure about the time, but it was still light when he had driven over. He had driven because of the rain. Usually he walked the few hundred yards along Van Brunt Avenue. Or rode his bicycle. He had driven in his—actually the parish's—station wagon. He had parked it in front of the church—an old white building which once had housed a Lutheran congregation. He had gone into the church to see to the things. He could not be sure how long he had remained inside. But when he came out again it was almost dark. So, sometime after five on that short day.

When he came out, there was no station wagon. And he was sure he had driven over.

"Father Armstrong's sort of an absentminded old guy," Asa had told Susan Heimrich. "But I guess he did drive over. Anyway, the wagon's not in the parsonage garage, where it's supposed to be."

"He's a dear old man," Susan said. "But he is absentminded."

The Heimrichs are not communicants of St. Mary's, but Heimrich knew Father Armstrong's reputation for absentmindedness. So did most of Van Brunt. He was also widely considered a nice old man, if needlessly high church. "All that folderol," one man had said to Heimrich once. Of course, the man who had said it had been a Baptist.

"If he parked in front of the church," Heimrich said, "the car would have been in plain sight from the street."

"He supposed it was," Susan said.

"Did he happen to remember whether he took the ignition key into the church?"

Asa had asked him that. Father Armstrong supposed he had. He always did. No, he couldn't lay hands on it in the church. But it had to be there somewhere. After all, the car belonged to the parish.

"Did he happen to remember anything about this parish station wagon? Its make? The year?"

He hadn't, offhand. But he had, after some research, found the registration certificate. The missing car was a 1971 Pontiac wagon. The license number and the motor number were on the certificate. Asa Purvis had telephoned both to the barracks. Presumably, the numbers had been added to the APB.

"Color of the wagon?" Heimrich asked Susan. "Does the old boy happen to remember?"

The reverend old boy had told young Purvis the car was a dark color. Originally, probably, a dark blue. Probably, yes, there were a few scratches on the finish. "Sometimes I do scrape into things, I'm afraid." It was still a good, serviceable car. "Faithful." Had it been wearing chains when the clergyman had left it in front of the church?

"Asa asked him about that," Susan said. "Asa's a good trooper, Merton. And he says Armstrong told him of course it had. He said he had them put on after Thanksgiving every year, and left them on until April. Because one can never tell."

"And an ounce of prevention," Heimrich said. "I hope Purvis told them to add, 'probably has worn down chains on rear tires' to the description."

Susan did not know.

Anybody driving along Van Brunt Avenue—or walking along it in spite of the driving rain—could have seen a 1971 Pontiac wagon standing in front of the church; if a local, could have recognized it; quite possibly could have guessed Father Armstrong had left the ignition key in it, whatever Father Armstrong supposed. And, of course, gone up to see. Somebody who had need of a big station wagon. Or, seeing one available, had conjured up the need.

"Michael thinks it would be nice if we had a tree," Susan said.

"We thought we might pick one up on the way home. And get the house warmed up. And turn off that damn oil stove. Now that the electricity is back on."

"Yes," Heimrich said. "And hoping it stays on."

Sometimes in bad weather—in very blowy weather—restored power is prone to relapse. Rural electricity is fidgety.

Susan and Michael and Michael's girl stood up.

"You'll be home for dinner?" Susan asked her husband. "After all, it is Christmas Eve."

"I'll try to be," Heimrich told her. "I'll try damn hard to be. The ornaments are in the attic, I think."

The Christmas tree ornaments were on the top shelf of the closet in Michael's room. Susan didn't bother to point this out. She said, "Yes, dear."

"We may need new lights," Heimrich said.

Susan knew they would need new lights. The old lights had given out, rather abruptly, two years ago, which was the last time they had had a tree, because it was the last time Michael had been home for the holidays. Susan said, "Yes, dear," and stood up.

She and the "kids"—who weren't really, of course—went from taproom to lobby. They came back almost immediately, and Michael was carrying Joan Collins's suitcases. Which meant that they had checked out of the inn. Which meant, presumably, that Joan was going to stay, at least over Christmas, with the Heimrichs. Which meant that somebody, probably Michael, was going to have to sleep on the living-room sofa. Or maybe not.

Susan waved as the three of them went out of the taproom to the parking lot and the car. Merton Heimrich blew her a kiss, as he often did when they parted. And, as always, the gesture embarrassed him a little. Hippopotamuses do not throw kisses.

Joe came over and they ordered. Forniss ordered beer with his food. Heimrich thought of milk. He also thought of hippopotamuses and ordered coffee. One thought leads to another. This did not, however, appear to hold true in relation to the problem of who had killed Samuel Jackson, Attorney and Counselor-at-Law.

They finished their cocktails while they waited for Forniss's hamburger and Heimrich's omelet. (Heimrich, with visions of a large mammal lingering in his mind, had toyed with the thoughts of a fruit salad. He had not toyed long.)

"There's always the matter of money," Forniss said. "It often enters in, M.L. Do we know how Jackson was fixed?"

They didn't, Heimrich realized. He had known Sam Jackson for a good many years, but never to the extent of knowing how Jackson was "fixed." Pretty well, he had assumed. Old families of the Hudson Valley usually were. (Susan's family was, a little unfortunately, an exception.) Jackson had, apparently, lived as he liked, which implied money. He had practiced law as he liked. Why, then, had he chosen to defend an apparently hopeless case?

"And," Forniss said, applying catsup to his hamburger, "who gets it? Always a point, isn't it?"

Heimrich said "Mmm" and put a fork in his omelet. It was rather overdone. He said, "We'll have to try and find out, Charlie. Bother Miss Arnold again after lunch. If she happens still to be at the office. Most people knock off early on Christmas Eve."

"Particularly if the boss is dead," Forniss said, and attacked his sandwich.

Alice Arnold was still at her desk in the outer office of Samuel Jackson, Attorney and Counselor-at-Law, when they got to it. This time they walked up to The Corners and crossed with the light. Traffic was heavy on the avenue. People doing last-minute shopping for Christmas presents, Heimrich assumed. Or for Christmas turkeys. Or just fleeing the city for the holidays.

Alice Arnold did not say, "You two again," except by the expression on her face. She said, "Good afternoon. You've thought of something else you want to ask me?" She had, Heimrich thought, been crying again.

The telephone on her desk rang and she answered it. She said, "Mr. Jackson's office, may I help you?" And then listened. She said, "We all are, Mr. Preston. It's an awful thing. Yes, it is hard to believe. I really don't know. Somebody'll be in touch with you." She hung up. "All morning," she said. "Calling to say how awful it is. Miss Gee about that will of hers. Clients and just—just people. I suppose there's nobody else they know to call."

"One of the things we wanted to ask you about," Heimrich said, "whom to notify—that sort of thing. Next of kin. We thought you might be able to help us."

She shook her head.

"His wife died some years ago," she said. "Perhaps there are in-laws. He never mentioned them to me. But why would he?"

Heimrich knew that Sam Jackson's wife had died some years ago. Ten or eleven years ago, he thought, and that Sam had not remarried. He knew that the Jacksons had had one son, and that the son had died in his teens. When you live in a community like Van Brunt, you get to know odds and ends about other people who live there.

"I think he had a nephew," Miss Arnold said. "A brother's son. James, I think his name is. Lives out West somewhere. James Jackson. Perhaps there will be more about him in the files. Mr. Jackson's personal files, that is. Only they're locked, I'm afraid."

"And you haven't a key to them, Miss Arnold?"

"Of course not. They're his private files. Why would I have, Inspector?"

"Well," Heimrich said, "you were his private secretary, Miss Arnold. Confidential secretary. Do you happen to know where he kept the key? None of the keys he had in his pocket looks right. Key to his house, of course. At least we assume so. And to his office here. And his car keys. Nothing that looks like a key to a file cabinet."

She looked at Heimrich for more than a minute before she said anything. Then she said, "Well, I don't think that I—that is, I'm not sure that I—" She stopped with that.

"Miss Arnold," Heimrich said. "Lieutenant Forniss and I are the police. We're investigating Mr. Jackson's death, because it's what we call a suspicious death. We'll take the responsibility. You do know where he kept the key?"

After a few seconds, she nodded her head. And her eyes filled with tears.

"It seems wrong," she said. "Prying into things he wanted to keep private. With him dead and not able to—to keep things private. Do you have to, Inspector?"

"Yes, I think we have to. The key, Miss Arnold?"

"On a little hook thing. Inside the top drawer of his desk. I'll——"

"We'll find it, Miss Arnold. You can come along if you like, but you don't have to. And anything we don't think is connected in any way with his death—well, we'll keep it private."

"Oh," she said, "I'll go with you, Inspector."

She led them again along the corridor. It was lighted, now. And the office fire had burned down to a few embers. It wasn't needed any longer. The big room was warm enough.

There were four filing cabinets behind the desk. Alice Arnold went behind the desk and opened the top right-hand drawer. She reached into it, without looking into it, and took a key off the little hook thing. She did not offer it to Heimrich. She said, "It's this one. I'll open it for you."

She turned to one of the file cabinets; the one nearest the desk chair. She did not sit in the chair, although that would have been more convenient. She turned the key in the lock and pulled open the top drawer of the four-drawer cabinet.

The top drawer held lettered separators. Heimrich pulled down the one lettered "J." It was only thinly separated from the one marked "K."

Samuel Jackson's birth certificate was in the space. He had been born in the village of Van Brunt, County of Putnam, State of New York, son of Jasper and Mary Jackson, in the year 1901. There was a marriage certificate. In 1925, Samuel Jackson and Margaret Horne had been united in marriage. "Horne" was a familiar name in Van Brunt, but a fading name. There had been Hornes when Merton Heimrich first came to live in Van Brunt. Timothy Horne and his younger brother, named—? Heimrich did not recall the brother's name. Both had died, within a year of each other, a few months after Heimrich had gone to live in Susan's house above the river. *The New York Times* had carried an obituary article about Timothy Horne. It had not been a long article, as Heimrich vaguely remembered it. He did not remember, even vaguely, what it had told about the life of Timothy Horne.

The same Horne family? Merton Heimrich could not see that it really mattered.

There was a letter, rather badly typed on an unheaded sheet of

typewriter paper. The typewriter keys had badly needed cleaning.
There was no address at the top of the sheet, and no date. It had
been written "Thursday." There was no telling what Thursday. At
a guess, from the look of the paper, a fairly recent Thursday. It
read:

Dear Uncle:
Thank you for your almost generous check. Believe me, I'm
sorry to keep bothering you, but there it is, isn't it? A ne'er-do-
well nephew, always in your hair. All right, things aren't
going any better for me. Things stay damn tight out here. The
shop pays about half enough to live on. I'm looking for something better, whether you believe it or not. So there we are,
aren't we? Anyway, thanks again.

Your "devoted" nephew,
James Worthington Jackson

Not a particularly friendly thank-you note. The quotation marks
around the word "devoted" constituted a sneer. Heimrich read the
letter again, and folded it and put it in his pocket. Alice Arnold
raised her eyebrows in disapproval. Heimrich paid no attention,
but went on sorting through the "J" section of the file. There was
very little else under "J." He skipped to "W." And found the will
of Samuel Jackson, duly witnessed by two people he had never
heard of; executed early in that year. And it was a copy. Original,
probably in a safe deposit box in the First National Bank of Van
Brunt.
It took only a minute or so to find a way through the legal ver-
biage.
Jackson had left fifty thousand dollars to Bertram Friday, "who
has been a faithful friend over so many years." "All the remainder
of the property both real and personal, of which I may die pos-
sessed" was to establish a trust for "my nephew, James Worthington Jackson, son of my brother, the late Paul Jackson." The First
National Bank of Van Brunt was to act both as executor and trustee. So. Fifty thousand dollars to one Bertram Friday. A nice round
sum, to Heimrich's mind. And the rest, however carefully tied up,

to his "devoted" nephew, who would get the income from the trust.

And what might that trust amount to? "Mmm." Some people surveyed their monetary value from time to time. Had Sam Jackson? If so, where would he have filed a summary? Under "M" for money? It was not. Under "M" there was only a thick bundle of letters, held together by a rubber band. Heimrich slipped off the band and looked at the bottom letter. It was dated twelve years ago. It was headed, "The hospital." It was hand-written. The writing was quavering, barely decipherable. The letter began, "Dearest love."

Heimrich confirmed what he already knew. The letter ended, "All my love, darling, Margaret."

He put it back in its place in the bundle of letters and snapped the rubber band around them. Some things are indeed private.

Not under "M" for money, which had been a ridiculous notion to begin with. The summary of net worth, if Sam had ever made one, had not been under "W" for worth; it was not under "N" for net. "E" for estate? Sam would never had used so stately a word. Or would he? After all, he had been a lawyer. He had not. Where, then, if anywhere? Probably, of course, nowhere. Heimrich had never listed his own assets—not his tangible ones. The others were fixed in his mind, primarily under "S" for Susan.

Heimrich stared down into the file cabinet. It seemed to stare back, as blankly. "P" for property? Seemed unlikely; turned out to be just that. "H" for—yes, by God, "H" for holdings. A large brown envelope with a sheet of white paper clipped to it. Written in pencil on the envelope: "Savings books, deeds, etc. Securities, custody Farthington, Brecht & Bernstein. (Steve Folsom.)"

Heimrich sat down in Sam Jackson's desk chair. (Alice Arnold's eyebrows went up again at this sacrilege.) He spread the contents of the big brown envelope on the top of the desk.

There were half a dozen savings bank certificates, issued by as many New York banks. All were for time deposits; all paid from $6\frac{1}{2}$ to 7 percent, compounded quarterly; one matured early in the coming January; the latest maturity date was four years in the future—almost four years. That account had been opened in the previous June when, presumably, Sam had thought he might have four years to live.

None of the accounts showed a total deposit of over forty thousand, but all were near that sum. Of course, top level for insured deposits. Heimrich totaled the deposits on a sheet of paper he found in the center drawer. (Miss Arnold was going to exhaust her eyebrows.) The total came to $236,737.96. Well, James Worthington Jackson was going to be able to give up the shop which paid so inadequately.

There were four deeds in the big envelope. One had yellowed with age. It transferred twenty acres, more or less, from one Hans van Fruylinghausen to Jacob Jackson, said land being situated in the Town of Van Brunt, Putnam County, New York. The transfer had been effective on the ninth day of April in the year of our Lord eighteen hundred and twenty-four. "To Jacob Jackson and his heirs and assignees forever."

The other three deeds were much more recent. Each assured Samuel Jackson (and his heirs and assignees) from twenty to thirty acres. The parcels adjoined one another. From the surveyor's maps, the hundred-odd acres—115, more exactly, and, of course, more or less—lay in a strip along the highlands above the Hudson.

Such land, Heimrich knew, was selling at around three thousand dollars an acre. The asking price sometimes reached five thousand. James Worthington Jackson wasn't going to have to have any job at all. Almost two hundred and forty thousand in banks, duly insured by the federal government; three hundred thousand, more or less—perhaps a good deal more—in land, if the bank, as trustee, decided to liquidate assets. And in custody of brokers? Might as well try to clear things up as they went along. If the brokerage firm hadn't shut up shop for the day. If Farthington, Brecht & Bernstein were in a cooperative mood. Or somebody named Steve Folsom happened to be. Which was very much an outside chance. Bankers and stockbrokers would no doubt talk only to each other—in whispers.

"Happen to know anybody there, Charlie?" Heimrich asked, and showed Charles Forniss what Sam Jackson had written on the outside of the big envelope. It was an off-the-cuff inquiry, of course. But Charles Forniss has a habit of knowing somebody almost anywhere.

"Nope," Forniss said. "Can't say I do, M.L. Farthington, Brecht and Bernstein. Nope. This Steve Folsom. Suppose he works there? Customers' man or something. I did know a Folsom once. Lieutenant in my outfit for a while."

Forniss's outfit had been the United States Marine Corps—Captain Charles Forniss, U.S.M.C.

"Could be, M.L., his first name was Stephen. With a P-H. But it's pretty vague. Long time ago, Korea was."

"Yes," Heimrich said. "A long time ago. And we're still there. We're still a lot of places, aren't we? Backing the wrong guys, a good deal of the time, wouldn't you say?"

"Three fourths of the time, for my money," Forniss said. "Come to think of it, it is my money. A couple of drops of it, anyway. Want me to try this Folsom guy? Old Marine buddy sort of thing. Probably the wrong Folsom, of course. Probably won't remember me if it's the right one. Value of Jackson's stocks and bonds in their vaults?"

"A rough figure will do, Charlie," Heimrich said. "Happen to have this brokerage firm's telephone number in your files, Miss Arnold?" He watched Miss Arnold's eyebrows. He was not disappointed.

She did have, in the card file in her office. But Mr. Jackson's private affairs were—

"A Manhattan telephone directory will do," Heimrich told her.

She said, "Bottom right-hand drawer, I think." There was relief in her voice. Her active participation into this prying was not required. Anybody can make available a Manhattan telephone directory.

Forniss found and dialed the number. He had to wait two or three minutes before he got "Farthington, Brecht and Bernstein good afternoon." The voice he got was a little blurred. It was also a little indignant. It didn't know if Mr. Folsom was available. All right, if it was that urgent, it would try to find out. "If you'll just hold on."

He held on for what seemed a long time. Heimrich worked through another drawer of Samuel Jackson's personal file. It was, so far as he could see, a waste of time. Well, detectives waste a lot of it. Part of the job. He did find under "E" a reel of 16mm film, in its original container. He left it where it was.

"Office party, probably," Forniss said. "He'll probably be—oh, hello, Mr. Folsom. You happen to be Lieutenant Stephen Folsom, U.S.M.C.?—Yeah, I know. So am I. Captain Charles Forniss in the old days. A cop now.—Yes, I did say 'cop,' Steve."

He listened for several minutes; Folsom's voice grated out of the receiver. Finally, Forniss said, "That would be swell, Steve. Only I don't get into town much nowadays. Yes, Steve. *State* police.— Well, I'm lieutenant, BCI. All right, Bureau of Criminal Investigation. Thought maybe you could help us a little, Steve."

He told Stephen Folsom how he could help and, briefly, what with. He said, in answer to something Heimrich could not overhear, "But the man's dead, Steve. Your firm will have to come through for the executors. Just trying to save a little time," and listened again. Then he said, "All right, off the top of your head, then. Roughly. As of closing yesterday. How much did you say?"

Forniss, who had been sitting in a client's chair at an end of Jackson's desk, reached a hand across it. Heimrich got a pad and a pencil out of the top desk drawer and put it in the waiting hand. Forniss wrote figures on it. He said, "O.K., Steve. Thanks a lot. Get back to the party, fellow. Yeah, I sure as hell will." He put the phone in its cradle.

"The right Folsom," Forniss said. "And I'll sure as hell look him up next time I'm in town. And the figures are just out of the top of his head, M.L."

The figures on the pad were $325,000–350,000.

Not too far under a million, add it all up. More than that, if they could get five thousand an acre instead of three. Plus, of course, whatever Jackson had in a checking account. Or several checking accounts.

James Worthington Jackson would be able to hire somebody to work for him—full time, if necessary.

Chapter 9

AT THE CORNERS, Forniss waited for the light to change and turned left into Elm Street, which had earlier been N.Y. 109 and would be again before it dead-ended a quarter of a mile, most of it almost straight up, from the Hudson River. There were no longer any elm trees on Elm Street. Through most of the country, elm trees had died away on the streets named for them.

The police car did not continue to the end of the narrow blacktop. After about a mile, Forniss turned right onto Van Brunt Pass, which was even narrower. There were pine trees on either side of Van Brunt Pass and they shaded it heavily. Ice still lay in patches on the pavement. If they stayed long enough on Van Brunt Pass— without skidding off it—they would be only a quarter of a mile or so from the Heimrich house, which was still known to most of Van Brunt residents as the "old Upton Place" (or the "old Upton barn"). Heimrich wished they were bound for it—for lights, if the power were really on, and warmth, with the same proviso, and perhaps a Christmas tree. It would be pleasant to have light. It was almost five in the afternoon and getting quite dark.

"Right along here," he told Lieutenant Forniss. "Sign's behind a bush. There!"

The sign, which was somewhat battered and almost hidden behind its bush, read "JACKSON." Forniss turned the car left onto a narrow roadway, thinly graveled and somewhat rutted. It did not look like a driveway to a millionaire's house. It looked like an almost abandoned farm road to nowhere in particular. It, like the pass, was heavily shaded. Like the pass, it had patches of ice on it. And as soon as they began to climb up it, they heard the tearing rasp of a chain saw somewhere ahead.

It was slow going up the long, steep driveway, and it was somewhat precarious going. It was understandable why, the night before, Sam Jackson had elected to stay in the comfortable warmth of his office, with his Aladdin lamps glowing, and to have his dinner at the Old Stone Inn. The drive swerved sharply, and the car skidded a little. Forniss checked the skid.

He was keeping his eyes sternly on the road, where they belonged. Heimrich could look around. So it was Heimrich who saw it and said, "Hold it, Charlie!" Charlie held it, although again it skidded to the sudden braking.

"There," Heimrich said, and pointed.

He pointed at a pull-off, cut into a tangle of underbrush—the beginning, or the end, of a narrow, dirt road. An old farm road, Heimrich thought; possibly an old hay road. But not, at least not entirely, an abandoned road. A car had been driven into it recently, and the wheels had cracked through ice and here and there dug into mud. And the marks of tire chains were apparent in the new-dug ruts.

"Funny place to stash a car," Heimrich said, and got out of the police car. And was thankful that he still was wearing the rib-soled country shoes. Somebody ought to invent shoe chains, he thought, and looked up the narrow dirt road, which was almost a dirt track.

Here and there, rays from the low, western sun fought in among the trees. And, a hundred yards or so in, sunlight glittered brightly from something. The glitter moved and flashed as the trees swayed in the wind. Forniss was beside him by the time he saw the glitter.

"Guess we'd better go have a look," Heimrich said, and the two tall men plodded up the track, occasionally skidding on ice and in mud. The glitter grew closer. Then they could see the car which had left its tracks in ice and mud.

Sunlight had reflected from the rear window of a big station wagon, with which the narrow road seemed to end. The station wagon was dark-colored—painted dark blue, as nearly as they could tell in the fading light. It was a Pontiac. It had no license plate. A big, abandoned Pontiac station wagon, stripped of its identity. Or was the word "hidden" more applicable? Not very well hidden, but a big station wagon is a little hard to hide.

"Well, well," Heimrich said. "Father Armstrong will be pleased, won't he? Get the parish wagon back. Eventually, that is." He tried to wedge himself in beside the abandoned wagon. There was not enough room between car and brush. Have to wait until Purvis had towed it out to see whether the parish station wagon had a scratch, with red paint embedded in it, on the right rear fender. A job for the lab boys, anyway.

The chain saw, which had been resting, started up again as they got back into the police car. Forniss had stopped on ice, and the car wanted to stay where it was and spin its wheels. Forniss let it fall back a little to get its wheels on gravel. There was no trouble after that, except for the grade and the sharp turns and, of course, more patches of ice.

"With all that money," Forniss said, "you'd think he'd have got himself a decent—" he let the needless sentence die a decent death.

They crept two or three hundred yards from the layoff before they came to a two-story white house—a house which, from the looks of it, had been standing there, high above the Hudson, for a couple of hundred years. It mildly needed painting.

A tree had fallen on the wide graveled area in front of the house. It was a big tree. In falling from its weight of ice it had missed the house by not more than a dozen feet.

A man with medium brown skin was standing by the tree, holding a chain saw. He wore a heavy windbreaker, almost a lumber jacket. The saw was resting on one of the limbs of the fallen tree— probably an ash, Heimrich thought—and the brown-skinned man had evidently been about to start it ripping through wood when the car pulled up.

He had already cut a considerable stack, fireplace length, of wood from the fallen tree. He laid the saw on top of the stack and turned to Heimrich and Forniss and said, "Good afternoon." There was no trace of Southern accent in his speech. There was a hint of inquiry.

He was a big man. Somewhere in his middle forties, Heimrich guessed. Two hundred pounds or so, and most of that bone and muscle. There was nothing especially Negroid about his face. At the moment, he was using the face to smile with. Heimrich said, "Mr. Friday?" and, in reply to a "Yes" and a nodding head, told him who they were. The smile went off of the brown face.

"About Mr. Jackson," Friday said. "Miss Arnold called and told me about it. A very bad thing, Inspector. A bad accident. Or—wasn't it an accident? I mean, with a police inspector involved. And a state police lieutenant?"

"We're trying to find out," Heimrich said, and Friday nodded his head again. "We wonder if you can help."

"If I can, I want to, Inspector. Mr. Jackson was a good man. I started sawing up this tree because he liked wood fires. Before I knew what had happened. Today—well, today I just went on sawing it for fires, although I guess now there won't be any. He was a good man, Inspector."

"Yes," Heimrich said, "I knew him, Mr. Friday. He was a good man. A good man to work for, I'd imagine."

"Oh," Friday said, "that too, Inspector. But I wasn't thinking of that, mainly. Just that he was a good man. Just good. Not in any special way. It's cold out here. You gentlemen like to come inside?"

It was cold. With the winter sun near setting, with the northwest wind still blustering, it was growing very cold. Things will freeze hard tonight, Heimrich thought; down into the teens, probably. Perhaps even lower. And colder still tomorrow; a cold Christmas, if not a white one.

Jackson led them into the house. It was warm in the house, although the wind rattled things, and made whining sounds at the windows. There was a fireplace in the square living room Friday led them into, and big logs were burning comfortably in it. But the fire was not really needed; electricity had reached Sam Jackson's old house. The ancestral Jackson house? Heimrich guessed it was.

"Sit down by the fire," Friday said. "Can I get you both something to drink?"

He himself remained standing.

"No, I don't think so," Heimrich said. "Sit down yourself, Mr. Friday."

Friday sat down; they all sat down—three big men in big chairs, in flickering firelight.

"Any way I can I want to help," Friday said. "You think it wasn't an accident, Inspector? Miss Arnold told me it was. That somebody—somebody who wasn't looking—backed a car into him at the inn. When he was going back to the office after dinner. It wasn't that way?"

"Pretty much that way, Mr. Friday. Only—whoever was driving the car may have been looking, we think. Looking very carefully. It was a big car, Mr. Friday. A big station wagon."

He watched Friday's face when he mentioned the wagon. He could see no change on it; the expression remained grave and attentive. It was not the expression of a man who knew that a station wagon, which probably was also a murder weapon, was tucked away in bushes some three hundred yards from where they were sitting. It was the expression of a man who was listening to a sad but interesting story and wondering about it.

"It doesn't seem possible," Friday said. "Somebody deliberately waiting to kill Mr. Jackson. Not Mr. *Jackson*." His voice shook a little on the repeated name.

"I'm sorry," he went on. "You see, he was more than a man I worked for—had worked for for more than ten years. I—well, I thought of him as a friend."

"The way he thought of you, apparently," Heimrich said. "What he called you in his will. 'Friend.' Did you know you were in his will, Mr. Friday?"

"He never said I was. Not in so many words."

"But you're not surprised?"

"I ought to say I am, oughtn't I? Sound better that way. But I can't, Inspector. No, I'm not surprised. You've seen his will, Inspector?"

"Yes, Mr. Friday. He left you fifty thousand dollars. The rest goes to a nephew, who apparently lives out west somewhere."

There was a change in the expression on Friday's face this time. His lips pursed a little, as if he had tasted something sour. "You've met his nephew?" Heimrich said.

"James Jackson. James Something-or-Other Jackson. Yes, he's visited here a couple or maybe three times since I've been here. Lives in Seattle, I think. Yes, I've met Mr. James Something-or-Other Jackson."

Heimrich waited for more. He didn't get it. "I take it," he said, "you weren't much taken by Mr. James Jackson? James Worthington Jackson, actually."

Friday got up and stirred the fire, which hadn't needed it. He sat down again. "Well, Inspector, he was Mr. Jackson's nephew. Son of his younger brother, who died some years ago, I understand. Mr. Jackson had been very fond of his brother, I think."

"Of his brother's son?"

"I wouldn't really know, sir. He didn't talk about his nephew much. To me, I mean. And James What's-His-Name never stayed very long. Only two days, the last time. Last June that would have been."

"Tell me something about him, Mr. Friday. How old is he about? What does he look like?"

"Twenty-five or so, at a guess, Inspector. Not very tall. Didn't look much like Mr. Jackson. Has yellow sort of hair and wears it pretty long. The way lots of them do, nowadays. I suppose you could say he's good-looking, if you like the type."

"As you don't, I gather?"

"Can't say as I does much, suh," Friday said. He had lapsed into dialect which was obviously a parody.

Heimrich thought a moment. Then he said, "Oh, he's that type, is he?"

"You could say that, Inspector. You could certainly say that." Friday had reverted to his normal speech after his brief venture into what amounted to Uncle Tomming. "The type that calls people 'boy.' People with my color skin. So—yes, you can say I'm prejudiced against the type, Inspector. We all have to be prejudiced against something, I guess."

"Don't have to be, Mr. Friday."

"All right, Inspector. Make it 'are.' No, I wasn't much taken with Mr. James Worthington Jackson. But not my business, was it? He was my employer's nephew."

"How did Mr. Jackson feel about his nephew? Didn't you gather anything? Get any feeling at all?"

"He never said anything to me about the boy. He wouldn't, would he? Not in so many words, anyway." He stopped, as if he had finished. He looked at the fire. When he spoke, it was as if he spoke to the fire. "You ask if I got any feeling about it," he said. "I guess I did. It seemed to me Mr. Jackson got uptight when his nephew was here; wasn't sorry when he left. But that could be because I got uptight myself. And, after all, you say he left James Worthington most of his money, so I suppose he got along with the boy better than I thought."

"Or," Heimrich said, "had nobody else to leave it to. Happen to know whether he had any other relatives, Mr. Friday?"

"If he had, he never mentioned them to me, Inspector."

"Last here in June," Heimrich said. "Only a couple of days, you say. Know where he went from here?"

Friday shook his head. He said, "Back home, far as I know. Back to Seattle. He'd flown to New York, way I got it, and rented a car at the airport. Drove the car back to the airport, I suppose. Got another plane to the West Coast. But that's just what I supposed, Inspector. Nobody told me anything."

"Probably the way it was," Heimrich said. "What time in June was he here, do you remember?"

"Toward the end of the month, way I remember it," Friday told him.

Heimrich could feel that Forniss was growing restless. Forniss believes in the direct approach.

Possibly Forniss was right.

"About this inheritance you're to get, Mr. Friday," Heimrich said. "You say Mr. Jackson told you—at least implied to you—that you'd be in his will. That you expected to be left something?"

"Yes."

"Did you know, I mean did he tell you, that it would be this much? Fifty thousand is a nice sum, isn't it? To me, anyway."

"To anybody, I'd think," Friday said. Now he looked directly at Merton Heimrich. There was no hostility in his regard. There was merely steadiness. "No, Inspector," he said. "He didn't mention any amount. No, I didn't think it would be that much. Are you going to say that people have been killed for less? Because I know they have, Inspector Heimrich."

Forniss came into it then.

"For the loose change in their pockets," Forniss said. "Let alone fifty grand."

Bertram Friday said, "Yes, sir." But he continued to look at Inspector Heimrich.

"Tell me about last night, Mr. Friday," Heimrich said. "You were here, in this house?"

"Yes. It wasn't a night to be out of a house, Inspector. Not if you had a house to stay in."

"No. Did anything happen? Anything out of the way?"

"A tree fell down," Friday said. "I thought at first it had hit the house. That must have been about ten o'clock. Maybe ten thirty. I'd been in bed a couple of hours. It woke me up."

"Begin earlier," Heimrich said. "I mean earlier yesterday evening. From, oh, about six on."

About six thirty, Samuel Jackson had called from the office. He said it was beginning to ice in the village and that he wouldn't try to make it home. That the power probably would go off, and that Friday was to try to keep the house from freezing up. That was all. "He didn't need to tell me to keep fires going," Friday said. "That was just—oh, something to say."

"He told you he was going to have dinner at the inn?"

"Didn't need to. What he often did when the weather was bad. Maybe he told me last night. More likely, he just assumed I'd know. He—well, he had habits, Inspector. Like most of us."

"Yes," Heimrich said. "So you kept the fire burning?"

"Fires, Inspector. There are four fireplaces in the house. It's an old house. Probably once fireplaces were all they had to heat it. I kept all four of them going."

"And?"

"Fixed myself something to eat. Ate it here by the fire. Read a while and—well, listened to the wind and the rain on the windows. Now and then went around and checked on the fires. Then the power went off, so I went up to bed. Set the alarm for midnight, so I could have a look at the fires."

"But you say the tree's falling woke you up before then?"

"Ten or ten thirty. I put some clothes on and went out to see what had happened. Found it had missed the house and I went back to bed, because there wasn't anything I could do about it until morning."

"During the evening. After around nine, say. You didn't hear anything else, Mr. Friday?"

"Just the wind howling. And the rain. And trees banging down a few times. It was a pretty noisy night, Inspector."

Heimrich agreed it had been a noisy night.

"Was there something you think I might have heard, Inspector? Something special?"

"Might," Heimrich said. "Just might. With the wind and everything, probably not. You didn't hear a car, Mr. Friday? Last night or this morning?"

Friday merely shook his head. But, as he looked at Heimrich, his eyes inquired.

"About halfway up the drive," Heimrich said. "A couple of hundred yards from the house, at a guess, there's a little side road. The remains of one, anyway. You know the place I mean."

"Yes. It leads—used to lead—to a sort of parking lot. Anyway, a cleared space where guests could leave their cars. Mr. and Mrs. Jackson used to give some pretty big parties, I understand. Had to have space for a good many cars to park. That was quite a while ago. Long time before I went to work for Mr. Jackson. What about this old road, Inspector? Pretty grown up now. And doesn't go anywhere. Not anymore."

"Some time last night or this morning," Heimrich said, "somebody drove a car into it. As far as the car would go. A big station wagon, Mr. Friday. Like, as nearly as the Lieutenant and I can tell, the one that was used to kill Mr. Jackson. It's pretty much wedged into the underbrush now. We'll know more when it's been dragged out. You don't know how it got there, Mr. Friday? How it got to be hidden there?"

"Where it would be sure to be found," Friday said. "Where I'd be the most likely person to have put it. Assuming I was half-witted. No, Inspector, I don't know how the station wagon got there. Or anything about it. Mr. Jackson didn't own a wagon. Never has. And I don't. He has—had—a Mercedes. Drove it to the office and wherever he needed to go. There's a Ford I use. For marketing. That kind of thing. No station wagon."

"This one," Heimrich said, "probably belongs to Father Armstrong. If it's the one we're looking for. By the way, Charlie——"

"Yep," Forniss said. "I was thinking of that, M.L. If Mr. Friday will show me where a telephone is?"

Friday would. Forniss called the barracks and told them they could stop looking for a dark blue Pontiac station wagon, and come and get it. And that they'd need a wrecker to get it out from where it was. And that the nearest wrecker was operated by Purvis's Garage. And that the lab boys were to go over it very thoroughly, with special attention to the rear end, and the right rear fender. And that, yes, he knew it was Christmas Eve.

Heimrich was standing up, with his back to the fire, by the time Forniss had finished telephoning. Bertram Friday was standing too.

"We'll be getting along," Heimrich said. "We'll probably be coming back. To go over any papers Mr. Jackson may have kept here at the house. That sort of thing."

Friday said, "Yes, Inspector."

"One other thing," Heimrich said. "You say—imply, anyway—that Mr. Jackson was a man of habit. Like going to the inn for dinner in bad weather."

"Yes, Inspector."

"Have you noticed any change in his habits recently?"

"Can't say that—well, there's this photography thing he's been going in for the last year or so. Home movies sort of thing. Never went in for that until—oh, last spring sometime. Mostly he took pictures of squirrels, birds, butterflies even. And old Woody. He's our resident woodchuck, Inspector."

"Ever run these movies off for you, Mr. Friday?"

"Sometimes."

"Was he good at picture taking?"

"Seemed all right to me, Inspector. Got some good shots of old Woody. Rambling off. Sitting up, looking innocent the way they do just before they eat up a garden. They walk funny, Inspector."

Heimrich knew that woodchucks walk funny, and that they eat up gardens. He had never thought them particularly photogenic. Except that all animals have moments of being so. Even human animals.

Bertram Friday went out of the house with them. He switched on a floodlight, set well up on the front of the house. It illuminated the parking area. They went to the police car; Friday went to his fallen tree. The shriek of his chain saw drowned the grinding of the car's starter. It followed them as they drove down the long driveway in the gathering darkness.

It was too dark to see the station wagon, deep in the stub of a road which had once given guests access to a cleared field where they could leave their cars for big parties given in gayer days by Margaret and Samuel Jackson. Sam Jackson had given no parties in the years Heimrich had known him. He had not attended many.

"As he says," Forniss said, as they neared Van Brunt Pass, "fifty thousand is a nice round figure. And where this damn wagon is ditched is an easy walk from the house. And last night wasn't a good one for long walks, was it? Where now, M.L.?"

"Yes," Heimrich said. "Anybody'd like to pick up fifty thousand. And it would have been a convenient place for Friday to have ditched the wagon. If, as he said, he was half-witted. Only, he doesn't seem so to me, Charlie. I'm going to knock it off for today, so you can drop me at home. Tomorrow we'll see what the lab boys make of the wagon."

Forniss turned the car left onto the pass. There were still patches of ice on the pavement. Thawing had finished for the day. The car skidded as he turned it up High Road. It wasn't a serious skid. Neither was the one at the turn into the Heimrichs' steep driveway.

"I'll call you at the barracks in the morning," Heimrich said, as he got out of the car. "We'll see what the lab boys come up with and where we go from there."

Forniss said, "Yep." He added that people are hard to get hold of on a holiday, especially when the holiday is Christmas. He drove away.

The raging wind tried to blow Heimrich down on his way to the front door of the house. It did not succeed. Hippopotamuses are hard to blow down.

Chapter 10

IT WAS BRIGHT AND WARM in the house. The fire was dancing on the fireplace; now something to look at, not to huddle in front of. They had found a tree—a symmetrical tree which reached almost to the ceiling. Susan had found the tree ornaments and got new strings of lights. One string was twinkling red and green. Colonel lurched to his feet when Heimrich went into the room. He looked at Heimrich mournfully. Mite came from somewhere to rub against Heimrich's ankles. Then he went to sit in front of the fire. Colonel lay down where he was, having, apparently, already overtaxed his strength.

Heimrich said "Hi!" and Susan came out of their bedroom. Heimrich took one look at her face and said, "What's the matter, dear?"

"It's all right, Merton," Susan said. "Everybody's all right, dear. Only I've been trying to get you, and at the barracks they didn't know where you were."

It was unlike Susan, who had grown used to a policeman's variable whereabouts. Something was wrong. Or had been wrong. She came across the room to him and he put his arms around her.

"We're all all right," Susan said. "Everything's all right. It really is, darling. Really."

"Only?" Heimrich said, and tightened his arms about his wife.

"Somebody shot at them," Susan said, and drew back a little so she could look up at him. "At Michael and Joan. They'd gone out so he could show her the river, with the sun setting on it. Only out on the terrace, dear. Only for a minute, because it's so cold and windy."

"Shot at them?" Heimrich said. "On the terrace? With what, Susan?"

"Michael thinks it was a rifle," Susan said. "From the Larkins' field, he thinks. The bullet hit a tree, he thinks. The big ash. Beyond where they were standing. It—it must have come close to them, Merton. Very close to Joan, they think. She says—well, that she could almost feel it, it was so close."

Air resists a bullet; a bullet stirs the air.

"You say Michael thinks the shot came from the Larkins' field," Heimrich said. "He didn't see who fired it?"

"No. They were looking at the river, they say."

"Side by side. Where are the kids, by the way?"

"In Michael's room. Joan's shaken up again, of course. As who wouldn't—"

She stopped, because Joan Collins and Michael came out of his room into the living room. Joan looked all right, except that, as they came in, she kept pushing back long hair which didn't, as far as Heimrich could see, need pushing back.

Michael said, "Hi, Dad. Mother's been trying to find you." Joan smiled. It was rather a tight smile.

"Your mother's told me what happened, Michael. You must think this is a violent village, Joan."

She smiled again. The smile was, Heimrich thought, a little more relaxed. She shook her head, but not with much resolution.

"From the Larkin land, you think, Michael."

"Pretty sure," Michael said. "From that little knoll. Where they used to have that weird little summer shelter with benches. Where nobody ever sat, as far as I can remember. They called it something strange. Something that sounded—oh, archaic, somehow."

"A gazebo," Heimrich said. "Something you can sit in and gaze out of. It blew down years ago. In a hurricane which came a little inland. And blew part of the roof off the old high school. The town hadn't insured against wind damage, because it never blows that hard here."

"I remember," Michael said. "We got an extra two weeks' vacation."

Conversations tend to wander. Heimrich put a curb on this one. He said, "You think it was a rifle, son?" That was what it had sounded like to Michael Faye. "Sort of sharp. Not hollow like a shotgun." But he was just guessing. "We were looking at the sunset. Or the start of the sunset. On the river. Behind the cliffs, you know."

Heimrich knew. He and Susan often sat on the terrace and watched the sun go down behind the highlands beyond the Hudson. But in the summer, not in weather like this.

"About what time was this, Michael?"

Michael thought it had been about four thirty. About then. They had just finished stringing the lights on the tree, and trying them out. One string hadn't lighted, but he had found the loose bulb and tightened it.

"Put a coat on," Heimrich said. "You can show me where you were."

There was nothing to check the wind which tore across the terrace. Fifty miles an hour, Heimrich thought the wind was blowing. Or what Charlie Forniss probably would call fifty knots. And it was very cold on the terrace.

"About here, we were," Michael said. "Joan was a little ahead. I was holding onto her shoulders, so she wouldn't blow away. We'd just stopped when somebody shot at us. From over that way." He turned and pointed.

Beyond the stone fence which marked the limit of the Heimrich land, the ground rose gradually. In one place it rose more steeply. That was the knoll Michael had mentioned; the one he now pointed toward. Heimrich took this from his memory; it was too dark to see anything beyond the reach of the terrace floodlight. It would have been about where Michael was pointing that the gazebo had stood. It would be about two hundred yards from the terrace. Within possible rifle range. By a good marksman, who might have allowed for lead time, and fired a little ahead of the moving couple. But they had stopped walking toward the outer edge of the terrace. Which might account for the fact that they were still alive.

"There was a sort of *clunk* sound," Michael said. "Why I thought it had hit a tree."

The big ash, which partly shaded the terrace from the summer sun, seemed probable as a stopping place for a bullet. It would have been in line with the knoll and the two standing on the terrace to watch the beginning of the sunset. Tomorrow, they could look at the tree for a place to start digging. It was too dark for that now; too dark and too cold. They went back into the house.

From the Larkin land, Heimrich thought, warming himself in front of the fire. But not by a Larkin. For one thing, the Larkins—Oliver and Olive Larkin, and their twelve-year-old son, Oliver, Junior—were in Florida, where they always were this time of the year. For another, Larkin was a notably mild man, not one likely to take potshots at his neighbors. And Oliver, Junior, would be allowed only an air rifle, if that. Oliver, Senior, had strong views on gun control. He notoriously wanted all firearms, including hunting weapons, licensed, if they could not be banned. He was not popular with the local chapter of the Riflemen's Association.

Larkin, whom Heimrich knew only slightly, probably hired somebody to keep an eye on the house during the annual migration to warmth. Palm Beach, wasn't it? Larkin was not a Miami Beach type. Fort Lauderdale? It didn't matter. From mid-December until mid-March, not Van Brunt. And somebody to check the house, to see that the furnace hadn't conked out and left the house to freeze; somebody to see that vandals didn't break in. But not, probably, to live twenty-four hours a day in the house, and to guard it against possible trespassers. Anybody, probably, could walk up the drive to the Larkin house, and go around it to the knoll. Or drive up to the house and carry a rifle from the car.

Or the caretaker could have had a shot at a woodchuck, always fair game for country people, and fired high. Except that woodchucks were sleeping in their burrows at this time of year; hibernating deep and warm, as sensible animals should in winter.

Almost time for before-dinner drinks. Entirely time for a shower. If electricity had been on long enough to heat the water; if Susan and the kids hadn't used up the hot water, outrunning the heater.

Under the shower, which started out hot enough, Merton Heimrich continued to speculate. It couldn't be more than speculation. There wasn't much substantial to go on. Somebody with a rifle. Somebody who was a fairly good shot; somebody, fortunately, who allowed for lead time. But how had this somebody known that Joan Collins and Michael Faye would go out onto the terrace on so cold and blowy a day to look at the sun declining behind the highlands beyond the Hudson River? No answer to that one.

The hot water suddenly turned cold. He'd got ahead of the heater. Or somebody had turned on the hot water somewhere else in the house.

Merton Heimrich got out of the shower.

Somebody had merely taken a chance; had just been hopeful. Somebody, then, who had felt a great need to kill. To silence. That was almost certainly it. Somebody who thought Joan Collins, looking out a window of the Old Stone Inn, had seen more than she had seen and had thought that no chance was too slim to take to see that she did not live to testify. And no exposure too arduous to be endured. The afternoon's wind would have been as harshly cold on an aspiring murderer as on a victim.

Somebody who knew the lay of the land and where to find a vantage point overlooking the terrace. Which meant almost any local. Or any past visitor at the Larkins'. Or anybody who had used the footpath along the ridge—the footpath which skirted the Larkin land and the Heimrich land, and, come to think of it, the Jackson land. The footpath which began where N.Y. 109 ended, and ran north from there for three or four miles along the high land above the Hudson. A pleasant walk in the summer, with a chance of cooling breezes. On a day like this, with the wind high and the sunlight ebbing, a rather brutal walk; one to be taken only in an emergency.

About four thirty, Michael thought it had happened. It had been a little after five when he and Forniss had found Bertram Friday sawing up a tree. Not more than a mile on the path. Plenty of time for a man in as good physical shape as Friday had seemed to be. And fifty thousand dollars is a pleasant amount of money. And the station wagon had been a convenient distance from Sam Jackson's old house. It had not been too effectively hidden; he and Charlie Forniss had proved that. But if they had driven up the driveway from the pass half an hour later, sunlight would not have glinted from the wagon's rear window. And the wagon could have been moved later to a less incriminating hiding place.

Presumably it had been moved by now; was being driven, or possibly towed, to the barracks and the lab boys, to whom Christmas Eve was merely another evening and Christmas Day merely another Thursday. Heimrich dressed in indoor clothing and went out into the living room. The Christmas tree twinkled at him. Susan and the kids were sitting in front of the fire. Susan was wearing her newest, and favorite, pantsuit; Michael had on a white turtleneck and a dark jacket. It almost looked as if he had dressed for dinner. And Joan was wearing a long skirt—a skirt, Heimrich noted, of many colors, all merging pleasantly to the eye. She wore a white jersey blouse above it. Heimrich could see what Michael had in mind.

None of them had glasses in front of them, although it was the time for glasses.

"We waited for you, dear," Susan said. "I'll get them now. I was going to have the turkey tonight, only it's still frozen hard as a rock. But I'm running cold water on the steaks to thaw them and they'll be all right under the oven broiler. It's too cold for charcoal."

She went to the kitchen, and ice began to tinkle.

Heimrich sat down. Mite came and sat on him. Colonel, lying in front of the fire, turned a heavy head to look at him. He's getting to be an old dog, Heimrich thought; for a Great Dane, a very old dog. With the wind in the northwest, the breezeway won't be too bad. With power on, and the starter, it won't take long to get the charcoal going. We'll have to see Friday again in the morning.

Probably I'll have to drive over to Carmel in the morning. They'll probably have visiting hours on Christmas Day. Not that that applies to me, of course. Peters won't be at his office. He'll be home with his family. On Christmas Day, nobody will be available.

Susan brought the drinks—martinis in a shaker for herself and Merton; bourbon and water in glasses for Joan and Michael; Joan's very pale. As ordered? Or was Susan being protective? It didn't much matter; at the moment, relaxed by his shower, warmed by the fire, Merton Heimrich felt too eased for much of anything to matter. For the moment. But only for the moment. Sam Jackson was dead. Sam had been a friend. Heimrich's concern was professional; it was more than professional. Sam had liked his martinis dry, very dry. He had made them so.

Merton Heimrich sipped his own.

"I'm afraid we're giving you a bad time here in Van Brunt, Joan," Heimrich said. "Letting you get chased off the road; getting you shot at. Van Brunt is usually more peaceful."

She was sure it was. "After all," she said, "he didn't hit me. There's that. Or Michael."

She looked at Michael. She had a warm smile for Michael; an endearing smile. She reached a hand out and put it over one of Michael's. She left it there. Kids aren't self-conscious anymore, Heimrich thought, and felt a little like an intruder.

"Anyway," Joan said, "it's a duty visit to my father. Stipulated by the court. He'll climb walls because I don't get there on time and, when I'm there, he'll forget all about me. Oh, he'd have taken me to dinner. At a very good restaurant. But I wouldn't really have *been* there, if you know what I mean. He would have been—just taking a daughter to dinner. *His* daughter, whose name is Joan. Not me." She sipped from her glass. "I'm probably not making any sense," she said. "Not any sense at all. Just making noises. Anyway, it's nice here. Peaceful, really. When we're not being shot at, that is."

There was a long pause. Then Michael and Joan started to speak at the same time. They both stopped and looked at each other. Michael said, "Sorry, baby."

"Nothing really," Joan said. "I'm just trying to say that you and

Susan are being very good to me, Inspector. And, I feel I'm—oh, horning in. Getting in the way. You were both surprised that I turned out to be a girl, weren't you? Expected that the friend who was driving him down would be another boy. He didn't tell you ahead, did he? Just sort of threw me at you. He's like that, sometimes."

Susan didn't really need telling what her son was like sometimes. She said, "If it was a surprise, it was a very pleasant one, dear. And you're not horning in. There you were just making noises, Joan. You don't have to, you know."

"All right," Joan said. "It was a silly thing to say. I suppose I'm uptight a little. What with everything."

"You've got a right to be," Michael said. "You've sure as hell got a right to be. This sniper, Dad. He was aiming at Joan, not at me, wasn't he?"

"I'm afraid so," Heimrich said. "Unless you——" The telephone interrupted. Heimrich went across the room to answer it. He spoke his name; he said, "Yes, Charlie?" and listened. He said, "Flat out?" and, after a moment, said "Mmm." Then he said, "Call it a night, Charlie," and then, after a moment, "Yes, I know it does. Good night," and replaced the receiver and came back to the fire and his drink.

"Charlie and I came across a station wagon at Sam's house," he said. "It may be the one that forced you off the road, Joan. They're taking it up to the barracks to look it over. It was more or less hidden when we found it. And Charlie says it was out of gas. Flat out. You know anything about this man Friday, Susan? Who worked for Sam?"

"Only that he worked for Sam, and that his name is Friday. 'My man Friday' Sam used to say. Oh, and that he's black. And that when Sam spoke of him it sounded as if he were fond of him."

"Yes," Heimrich said. "Seemed to be fond of him. He left him money in his will. Quite a good deal of money."

Susan said, "Oh."

"Yes," Heimrich said. "It's a possibility. You run across him, Michael?"

"If he's the man who helps get the club courts set up in the spring, I have, sort of," Michael said. "Just to know his name. Seemed like a nice enough guy. If it's the right guy, that is. Unless I what, Dad?"

Heimrich said, "Huh?"

"You started to ask me something," Michael said, "when you were saying it was Joan who was shot at. Unless I—and then the phone rang."

"Nothing," Heimrich said. "Oh, unless you know something you haven't told me about."

"No," Michael said. "What would I know? I didn't see this station wagon back into Mr. Jackson."

"No," Heimrich said. "I'm afraid Joan was the target. Unless it was some goon shooting at random. At a rat, or something."

"It would have to have been a pretty tall rat," Michael said. "Maybe aiming at something in a tree, I suppose. But you don't think so, do you?"

"No," Heimrich said, "I'm afraid it was you two. Miss Collins, I'm afraid it was."

He finished his drink. He was, he realized, drinking faster than the others. There was no reason he should be. He wasn't going any place, except, after a while, out to the breezeway to get the charcoal going. It would be cold in the breezeway; outdoor cooking was for summer; for terraces and patios and picnics. But steaks should be cooked over charcoal; his wife was about to be overruled.

Susan had seen his empty glass. She emptied her own. She went to the kitchen and, again, ice cubes rattled in glass. She brought the shaker back, and two freshly frozen glasses. Heimrich twisted lemon peel and rubbed the edges of the two cold glasses; he poured into them. She had, as always, made precisely two. He twisted the peel over the drinks, and tiny droplets of oil appeared on the surface of the liquid—appeared and disappeared. Merton and Susan Heimrich clicked their glasses together.

"Picnic." The word, which had entered his mind for some reason—of course, steaks broiled at picnics—remained in his mind.

"Unless," Heimrich said to Michael, "you were at this picnic of the Lords' last summer. Saw something there."

"I wasn't," Michael said. "On the Fourth, I was playing tennis at the club. Finals of the men's tournament. First round of eight this year. Heat waves discourage people sometimes. Lord did say something about my dropping around. Said he knew his father would be glad to have me. Something like that."

Michael had remained in Putnam County the summer before, while his parents were in Europe. He had got a summer job on the Cold Harbor *Advocate*, a weekly which, in the main, advocated right-wing Republicanism. Michael had been what amounted to a copyboy. He had not been, Heimrich gathered, particularly enamored of journalism as a possible vocation. He was still thinking of being a tennis pro, which would be more fun and would, he gathered, pay better.

"If I had gone to this picnic," Michael said, "what would I have been supposed to see? That would make somebody shoot at me?"

"Nothing, I guess," Heimrich told him. "Lord was killed at his picnic. Sam probably was there. Now Sam's been killed. Two dead men. That's the only connection. Not much of one, naturally. You know young Lord, then? Burton Lord's son?"

"Met him, once or twice. He's Lord's stepson, actually. His father was named Nolan. George Nolan, I think it is. Mrs. Lord's first husband, way I get it. Former husband, anyway. Lord adopted Alan——"

"Yes," Heimrich said. "Mrs. Lord told me. You don't know Alan Lord well, I gather? About your age? Is that right?"

"I guess so, Dad. Junior at Cornell, I think he is. I've just—oh, met him around. Not often. I did go up to his place once. Some time last June, I think it was. They've got a tennis court. Like a lot of people with private courts, they have to fish for players. Good court, and Lord had a gardener or something to keep it up. Only it's got tape markers, and you hit the line, any line, you get pretty weird bounces."

"You went just that once?"

"Yeah. Way Alan put it, they ask guys once. If they turn out to be good, that's the end of it. If the guy's too bad, same thing. Four other guys around the day I was there. All bunnies."

A "bunny" to Michael is somebody who plays tennis badly.

"So you weren't asked back?"

"No. Better competition at the club. Not that it's all that hot. Oh, Ted Holcomb's good enough, or almost. Anyway, we always seem to meet in the finals. Carried me to three sets on the Fourth. His serve conked out in the third, though. Broke him in the second game and after that he just—well, sort of wobbled. Third game I——"

Tennis players are a little like golfers. They, too, tend to replay games vocally, particularly, of course, those they have won.

"I take it," Heimrich said, "that Alan Lord isn't much of a player?"

"In a word, lousy. No backhand at all, and you can murder his first serve. Nice enough guy otherwise, far as I know. Bit of a weirdo, from what I hear. Longhair type. But that's all right. Some of the guys at Dartmouth let it grow long."

"Long enough to braid, some of them," Joan Collins said. "And beards. You never saw such beards, Inspector. Dad says that, with all that hair, you can't see their faces well enough to tell whether they're still awake. He thinks that, most of the time, they're not."

Collins, Heimrich noted, was always, formally, "Father." Her stepfather was "Dad."

The conversation was wandering far from the subject, if there had ever been a subject. He put on a heavy coat and went out to the breezeway. Shivering only slightly, he poured charcoal briquettes into the bowl of the broiler and put the electric starter on the charcoal and poured more briquettes on top of it and plugged it in. He went, thankfully, back to the fire and his diminished drink. It was, certainly, cold out for outdoor cooking. But Susan had found a butcher who still had, at intervals, prime beef, and only charcoal could do justice to his steaks.

Heimrich lingered over his second drink, giving the charcoal time. He got up once and propped the steak board in the fireplace to heat. When he finished the drink, he went to the kitchen door which opened on the terrace and looked out through its glass panel. The charcoal glowed red. Electric starters are admirable. When, of course, you have electricity. Much superior to lighter fluid, which often burns off, igniting only itself. Heimrich put his heavy coat on again, switched on the breezeway light and got the steaks. They were thick strip steaks, and not yet at room temperature, as recommended. Whatever "room temperature" is supposed to be.

He went out to the breezeway and smoothed the glowing charcoal level. He lowered the grill so that it was only three inches or so above the coals. He put the steaks on and they sizzled. He stood to the lee of the broiler so that the heat would blow toward him—not that, now, the wind was more than a breeze on this side of the house.

Fat dripped from the steaks and flared into flame on the charcoal and enveloped the steaks. Which, contrary to legend, would do the steaks no harm. When he decided it was time, he flipped the two thick steaks over. He went back into the living room and got the steak board, which ought to be warm enough by now.

Outside again, he raised the grill until it was almost a foot above the fire. He took one of the fire-crusted steaks off the grill and laid it on the board. He and Susan liked their steaks rare. The kids had specified medium. Nice kids, for all that. He went back to the third drink, which he knew Susan would have ready.

She had waited to pour them into refrozen glasses. Somebody, probably Michael, had resupplied the bourbon drinkers. "Must be cold out there," Susan said. "I could have done them in the oven. I do them quite well in the oven, dear."

Merton Heimrich said, "Mmm." He said, "Not too cold."

When he had half finished his drink, he went out and put the steak destined for rareness back on the grill. He went back and finished his drink, not hurrying with it. When he had finished it he went back to the breezeway and pushed a long-tined fork into one of the steaks. He flipped both of them over again. Yeah. He opened the door and said, "O.K." to Susan, who was forking open baked potatoes. He carried the steaks to the kitchen and sliced them, and sorted slices onto hot plates. The rare ones were rare; the medium ones medium. Well, medium rare.

They ate in the dining section of the long living room, which was some distance from the fire. Mite joined them and spoke at length about people who starved cats.

They tried television after coffee and fruitcake, but television was full of jingle bells and people standing in snowstorms singing carols. After "Silent Night, Holy Night," Michael carried blankets from his room and made up a bed on the long sofa. Nobody had suggested this, although both Susan and Merton had wondered. When jingle bells, jingle bells started up again, they all went to bed, although it wasn't quite ten o'clock. Joan said, "Good night," as she went into Michael's room. She did not say, "Good night all," an abstinence of which Heimrich approved. And she did not, as far as he could hear, lock the door behind her.

Chapter 11

MERTON HEIMRICH woke up early. The sun was not up yet, but somewhere a church bell was ringing. St. Mary's and a call to the faithful for early mass? Probably. It was "mass" at St. Mary's. Heimrich shaved and dressed and went out to the living room. Michael had kept the fire up through the night. He was sitting near it and reading a book. He had folded the blankets neatly and put them on the end of the sofa and put the pillow on top of them. Apparently he had fluffed up the pillow. It showed no indentation of a head. Neat young man, Michael.

Michael's hair looked slightly damp, as if he had recently taken a shower. There were only two showers in the house, and the other was in the bathroom off Michael's room. It's none of my business whether he did sleep on the sofa, Heimrich thought. He could have held his head under a faucet in the half-bath. He said, "Morning, son." He could not help adding, "Make out all right on the sofa?" although that was none of his business either.

Michael said, "Fine, Dad. I made some coffee. Joan isn't awake yet."

Heimrich said, "Good. She needs the sleep. After what she's been through," and went to the kitchen and poured himself coffee from the Chemex, keeping warm on an asbestos sheet over an electric burner set at SIM. Michael had learned his way around when he had been alone in the house last summer. He had learned to make good coffee.

Merton had a second cup while he waited for his egg to boil and the toast to pop up. He made more coffee for Susan and the girl from Hanover and ate toast and egg in the kitchen. It was only eight thirty. Too early to call Charlie Forniss at the barracks. Charlie might even be a little late, considering it was Christmas Day. Heimrich rinsed out his eggcup and poured himself another cup of coffee and put the Chemex back on its asbestos pad. He carried the coffee into the living room and sat by the fire. Michael was still alone in the room. He was still reading a book. Heimrich lighted a cigarette and held the pack out toward his son.

Michael shook his head. He said, "Given them up, Dad. Supposed to be bad for the wind."

Merton could hear Susan stirring in their bedroom. Then he could hear the shower running, which surprised him slightly. Susan usually showered in the evening, as he did. Special for Christmas, probably. He drank coffee and smoked and listened for sounds from Michael's room. He heard none. Joan Collins was really sleeping in. He wondered if Michael had actually spent the night on the sofa. One cannot help wondering about things. Were the kids being considerate of the supposed prejudices of aged parents? It was only a few steps from sofa in the living room to the unlocked door of Michael's room.

When I was Michael's age, would I have slept sedately on a sofa with a girl so near—a waiting girl? Heimrich thought. If, say, the girl had been Susan Upton? Years, too many years of course, before he had met Susan, who hadn't been Upton when they met; Susan, who hadn't any longer been Upton. Idle speculation, of course. And about a matter he couldn't consider important. Perhaps Susan could. He doubted that.

Susan came into the room. She was wearing a pantsuit. Usually, at breakfast time, she wore a robe. For Christmas, probably. Susan said, "Good morning, darling. Son. And Merry Christmas, of course."

"Merry and frigid," Michael said. "It was ten above when I got up. But not as windy. On the phone they say partly cloudy with a chance of snow flurries. Joan's still asleep, Mother. Do you think we ought to wake her up?"

"She'll need all the sleep she can get," Susan said. "After her introduction to Van Brunt. Did either of you two think to leave some coffee?"

"We both did," Heimrich told her. "It's keeping hot."

"You're dears, both of you," Susan said, and went into the kitchen for coffee.

Heimrich looked at his watch. Charlie Forniss was due at the barracks, Christmas or no Christmas. He finished his coffee and stubbed out his cigarette. Susan came back, carrying her cup, as he lifted the telephone. She said, "I suppose there's no point in telling you it *is* Christmas, Merton dear?"

"I'm afraid not much," Merton Heimrich said. "Since it's still murder." He dialed the barracks.

Yes, Lieutenant Forniss was in his office, Inspector. Just a moment. And Merry Christmas.

Forniss said, "Morning, M.L." He didn't mention Christmas. He didn't expect it to be merry.

"We're splitting up today," Heimrich said. "Send somebody down to dig a bullet out of the big ash by the terrace, will you? It will be too smashed up to be of any use, probably. Have it sent to the lab, anyway. Have they finished going over that wagon of ours, do you know?"

Forniss didn't. He had just got in; he had been just about to check with the lab boys. If M.L. wanted to hang on?

Heimrich didn't. Lunchtime would be soon enough. At the inn. About one, say. Forniss pointed out that lunch that day would be Christmas dinner, probably starting at noon. Did Heimrich want Christmas dinner at noon? And what was this about a bullet in a tree?

"Fill you in at lunch," Heimrich said. "Meanwhile, Charlie—"

It took several minutes to tell Charlie Forniss the meanwhiles. Forniss said, "O.K., I'll get at it. And you, M.L.? If, say, I run into somebody who wants to confess all? Not that I will."

"Not that you will," Heimrich agreed. "I'll be at Carmel. At the county jail probably. Or, possibly, at the D.A.'s office."

"District attorneys don't work on Christmas, M.L. Only cops work on Christmas. And maybe bus drivers and subway crews. See you at the inn. We'll hope there'll be room there."

Heimrich put the telephone back in its cradle. He looked at Susan, who probably had overheard what he had told Forniss about going to Carmel, county seat of Putnam County.

Susan had. Susan said, "Damn."

Joan Collins came out of Michael's room, and Michael stood up and his face lighted up. She said, "Merry Christmas, Michael. And to both of you. I had a wonderful sleep. Didn't even turn over all night. And isn't it a beautiful morning?"

She, too, had dressed up for Christmas. She was wearing a green and gold robe, and had tied back her long hair. She certainly wasn't the "boy" they had expected. And if she said she had slept the night through without turning over, she had slept the night through without turning over. It was, of course, mildly interesting that she had thought to mention it.

"Is there coffee?" Joan said.

"Of course, dear," Susan said. "And juice and whatever else you want. Within reason, of course. Bacon. Eggs. The usual things."

"I'll come and help," Joan said.

Susan has a rather marked lack of enthusiasm about offers to help in the kitchen. Volunteers have to be told where everything is. They also tend to get in the way. Heimrich, knowing this, was a little surprised by the smiling readiness with which Susan accepted the offer.

He went into the bedroom to put on city clothes, appropriate for a visit to a county jail on Christmas Day. Again in the living room, where now everybody was having breakfast, Heimrich said he'd be back when he could. Susan said she hoped it would be earlier than that, and Heimrich went through the kitchen and across the breezeway to the garage. It was very cold in the breezeway; it was also still a little icy. The Buick started reluctantly. Newish cars are lethargic cars. Heimrich thought wistfully of the Skylark, GS, they had had until the brakes failed—failed three times, and always with Susan driving. It had, understandably, given her a block which not even a new master cylinder had dissolved.

He drove down the steep driveway and south on N.Y. 11-F and then east toward Carmel. He started in sunlight, but after the first few miles the sun vanished and it began, heavily, to snow. A flurry, of course. The blustery wind was from the northwest. Real snow came with the northeasterly. Only a flurry, Heimrich assured himself, trying to see through it. Snow blew across the pavement; the wipers fought snow. Finally, the heater began to fight against the cold. The wind continued its effort to blow the Buick off the road, a not very wide blacktop, with a few patches of ice still on it. Heimrich thought of Gilbert's comment on the policeman's lot. He also thought he could have put Carmel, and an interview with Loren Kemper, off a day. Not that tomorrow would likely be much better.

He turned on the radio for the ten o'clock news. The President, in a speech in Denver, not too far from where he was having a "working vacation" at a ski lodge, had appealed for national unity. He had spoken strongly against divisiveness. He had said that he sought to cooperate with Congress on energy, but that cooperation was a two-way street.

The weather service started with a cold-wave warning, temperatures dropping to near zero in the city and ten below or lower in the normally colder suburbs. Tonight would be very cold, but with diminishing winds. The outlook for Friday was for partly cloudy and windy, with a chance of snow flurries.

Just before he reached Brewster, the current flurry stopped and the sun came out, blindingly in his eyes. North of Brewster on the way to Carmel it had been snow the night before, instead of freezing rain. The road had been scraped. Yes, it had been freezing rain first and then snow. But the metal studs bit in. For the most part, anyway. It was almost noon when he reached Carmel. He had underestimated the weather when he had told Charles Forniss one o'clock would be all right for meeting at the inn. But Charlie, too, probably would have a long morning.

There was a guard in the courthouse lobby. No, District Attorney Jonathan Peters was not in his office. Neither was the Chief of County Detectives, although there probably was somebody on standby in that office. It was Christmas. Hadn't the Inspector noticed?

"And a lousy one," Heimrich noted, and went to the jail.

The head guard was also taking Christmas off. But there was a deputy who, after considerable hesitation, supposed it would be all right for Inspector Heimrich to interview Mrs. Loren Kemper. "Although it's about time to feed them."

Loren Kemper, who was brought into a barren room, after a considerable wait, by a matron, was a slim, noticeably pretty woman somewhere in her mid-twenties. She had an almost boyish figure. She was wearing a close-fitting gray wool dress. Her golden-yellow hair, almost, but not quite, as long as the brown hair of Joan Collins, hung loose. There was no friendliness in the blue eyes which looked at Heimrich.

"I won't talk to you or anyone without my lawyer," Loren Kemper said. "He says I've already talked too much to that Cochran man."

Heimrich knew Leon Cochran, Chief of County Detectives. He thought Cochran a man rather likely to get underfoot. He told the matron she could leave. The matron, a very heavy-set woman with almost black hair and a very visible mustache, also black, said, "Not allowed, Mister."

"Yes," Heimrich said, "I'm allowing it, Miss. I'll be responsible."

The matron said she'd have to see about that, but she went out of the room, presumably to do so.

"Your lawyer was Mr. Jackson," Heimrich said to the slim woman, who remained standing, and remained hostile. "Samuel Jackson?"

"I don't know why you say was," Loren said. "He is my lawyer, whoever you are."

Heimrich told her who he was. He said, "Because Mr. Jackson is dead, Mrs. Kemper. He was killed night before last, under rather puzzling circumstances. And he was a longtime friend of mine, Mrs. Kemper. A friend whose judgment I very much respected."

She said, "Oh." Then she sat down on one of the three very unwelcoming chairs in the barren room. "He's really dead? Nobody told me. You'd think somebody would—" She put her hands over her eyes. "He was a nice man," she said. "A kind man. What do I do now?"

Now, he told her, she'd have to think about finding another lawyer. When she found one he would, undoubtedly, move to have her trial postponed. The motion would, equally without doubt, be granted. "So your new lawyer will have time to familiarize himself with the case."

"I don't know anything about lawyers," she said. "Not even how to go about finding one."

"You found Jackson," Heimrich told her.

She shook her head.

"It was the other way around," she said. "There was another one first. When they said I was a material witness and would have to put up bail or—or be locked up—the first one fixed up the bail and got me out of there. He said he would represent me, but I don't think he wanted to much. Then Mr. Jackson offered to. He called and offered. I thought—just vaguely thought—lawyers weren't allowed to do that. But I wasn't a witness at all. Not material or anything. I was out by the pool when it happened. When somebody shot Burton." She covered her eyes again and murmured something. Heimrich thought it was "Burton, oh Burton," but he couldn't be sure.

"Just called you up and offered to represent you?" Heimrich said. "Yes, I suppose the county bar association might take a dim view. Call it advertising, or something. Lawyers are getting a little touchy about ethics since Watergate. Did Jackson say why he made this offer?"

"No. Just said he'd be glad to represent me. And it was all right with the other lawyer—he'd cleared that up before he called me. And he said I wasn't to worry."

"Did he tell you why you didn't have to worry, Mrs. Kemper?"

She shook her head.

"Just not to. That he was sure things would come out all right."

"Did he say why he was sure?"

"No."

"You didn't ask? Try to find out why he was so confident? Why, more or less out of a clear sky, it seems, he offered to represent you?"

She shook her head again, her long hair sweeping her shoulders.

"You don't understand," she said. "I was upset, terribly upset. Not about myself. I knew I hadn't done anything. That Burton was dead. Dead in that awful way."

"You were fond of Mr. Lord?"

She looked up at him, surprise in her eyes.

She said, "Fond? You don't seem to know much about any of this, do you, Inspector? That's why I'm here, really. And what this man Peters saw, or thinks he saw. Burton and I were lovers. I don't deny that. Sleeping together. I don't deny that. That's why they think I killed him. That we'd been lovers and—well, he decided to call it off. He didn't. Oh, it was called off all right. But that was my idea. Because what had been bright was getting—messy. Not between us. I don't mean that. But his wife had hired a detective—some dreadful man—to spy on us. We'd—well, we'd have to take to hiding around corners. I suppose Mrs. Lord thought she had a right to hire a man to spy on us. Maybe she did, I guess. The way a woman like Amelia Lord would look at it. She was so proud—so set up—about being Burton's wife. And having all that money he'd made. She's that kind of woman, I think."

Heimrich waited a few seconds for her to go on, but it became evident she had gone as far as she intended to.

"How long had this been going on, Mrs. Kemper? This affair of yours and Mr. Lord's?"

"Since—oh, about two years after my husband died," she said. "At first, well, I was just lonely. Terribly lonely. Later it got to be—well, something different. Why are you asking me all these things? Things that man Cochran asked me over and over? Until I felt like screaming. You're trying to trap me into something, aren't you? Taking advantage of the fact Mr. Jackson's dead to trap me. How do I know you're not lying about that? About his being dead?"

"He's dead, Mrs. Kemper. We think somebody killed him,

meaning to kill him. I'm not trying to trap you. Just to see whether there's any connection between what we think was Sam Jackson's murder and the murder of Mr. Lord."

"What connection could there be, Inspector?"

"I don't know. I'm trying to find out. We look for anything out of the way in the past of a murder victim, you see. Sam Jackson never practiced criminal law, far as we can find out. But he offered to be your attorney in a murder case."

She shook her head. "I can't see why that would make any connection," she said.

"Probably there isn't any, Mrs. Kemper. We try to cover all possibilities, naturally. It was your rifle used to kill Mr. Lord; I understand you don't deny that?"

"It was my gun. The one I used for target shooting at the club. And I kept it in the hall closet. All anybody would have to do would have been to open the front door and reach in while I was out by the pool. I told this Cochran man that, too. He wrote it down, but I don't think he really listened to anything I said."

Heimrich supposed that Chief of County Detectives Leon Cochran had listened. Which didn't mean he had believed anything he heard.

The door to the barren room opened and the matron came in, her mustache perceptibly quivering.

"If you want your dinner you'll have to come and get it," she said. "Makes no difference to me. It's turkey, on account of its being Christmas." She glared at Mrs. Kemper. She had glare left over for Inspector Heimrich.

"Turkey and all the fixings," she said, as Heimrich had been sure she would. "Special on account of Christmas. You coming?"

The matron moved a step farther into the room. The step symbolized a resumption of the authority of which she had, momentarily and unfairly, been deprived. It would show a state police inspector.

Loren Kemper went with the matron.

Heimrich went out to his car. It hadn't got any warmer. But the sky was relatively clear and the air tasted better. It didn't taste of disinfectant. And the Buick, perhaps invigorated by the freshness of the air, had thrown off its lethargy. The engine took the first hint.

It didn't take as long to drive back to Van Brunt as it had taken to get to Carmel. Still, it was after one thirty when Heimrich went into the taproom of the Old Stone Inn. Forniss was there, waiting. So were a good many other people. Joe Shepley was busy. Forniss, like most of the others in the room, had a glass in front of him. He was at a corner table for two. It was a little, but not much, secluded. There was a briefcase on the floor by Charles Forniss's chair.

Shepley, behind the bar, held a martini mixer up and gestured with it. Heimrich nodded his head to Shepley and sat down. Forniss raised his eyebrows.

"Sam Jackson offered his services to Mrs. Kemper," Heimrich said. He said "Thanks" to Shepley for a chilled glass and a miniature milk bottle of martini. He twisted lemon peel over his drink and dropped the spent peel in the ash tray. "She and Lord were having an affair. Mrs. Lord was onto it. Mrs. Kemper kept her rifle in a hall closet near the front door. She had it partly for protection, partly for target practice at the club. She didn't kill Lord. She's having turkey and what they call, what the matron calls, anyway, 'all the fixings' for dinner. Dinner at noon."

"Pretty much what they'll give us here," Forniss said. "If we have lunch here. Maybe we can wangle a turkey sandwich. She admits she and Lord were sleeping together? What Peters will use as a motive, you know. Jealous rage of a rejected woman. She told the county boys the same thing about the rifle. Twenty-two target rifle it is. A good one, one of the county boys tells me. And she's a good shot. Friend of mine at this club says she was tops. Among the women, anyway. Why do people join rifle clubs, M.L.? So they'll be able to hit Indians?"

"Or rapists, I guess."

"The knee's better," Forniss said. "Anyway—"

Anyway, James Worthington Jackson did live in Seattle. He had no record with the Seattle police. He owned a small electric appliance shop. So far as Seattle had found out by a quick check, it was not only small but getting smaller. Jackson was thought to be in his middle or late twenties. He was not married. He had an apartment above his shop. It, too, was small. He owned a three-year-old station wagon. Yes, a Pontiac wagon.

Jackson was not in town. There was a sign on the shop door which read "CLOSED FOR THE HOLIDAYS." He had said he'd probably be gone a couple of weeks. The police didn't know. He had not said where he was going. He had gone in the Pontiac station wagon, apparently. At least, the wagon was not in the shed behind the shop, where normally it lived.

Forniss had had no trouble in getting into Samuel Jackson's office, using a key requisitioned from the property clerk at the barracks. He had had no trouble in finding the key to Jackson's private file cabinet, which was on the hook in the desk drawer, to which Alice Arnold had returned it. Miss Arnold had not been in the office. She was at home.

"Mourning, I guess," Forniss said.

Heimrich agreed that Miss Arnold probably was mourning—mourning a man and, possibly, the extinction of a wistful hope.

Forniss had had no trouble finding Jackson's checkbook registers for the last three years. The most recent showed a balance in the First National Bank of Van Brunt of—Forniss took a folded sheet from his jacket pocket and looked at it—of $5,126.83. "Only," Forniss said, "it's actually a hundred dollars less than that. He didn't add too well."

"A lot of us don't," Heimrich said, and Forniss said, "I balance to the penny, myself. And probably waste a lot of time. Anyway—"

Anyway, Jackson's deposits in his checking account averaged about fifteen hundred a month, sometimes more and sometimes less. There was nothing to indicate the source, or sources, of these deposits. Probably, Forniss thought, checks from his brokers.

The stubs showed checks drawn to "J.W.J." They were also in varying amounts, ranging from seven hundred fifty (and no cents) to two thousand. The most recent stub, which was for the two thousand, was dated the thirtieth of the preceding June. Forniss had not yet had time to go through the monthly envelopes of statements and canceled checks. "Got them all there," he said, and pointed down at the briefcase on the floor.

He also had there the roll of 16mm motion picture film. He had found it, as Heimrich had told him he might, behind the "E" divider. "Probably meant to put it in the 'F' spot," Forniss guessed. "Missed it by a letter."

"Probably," Heimrich said.

"So," Forniss said, "I went on over to see Jackson's man Friday. He——"

"Hold it a moment, Charlie. About Jackson's nephew. The Seattle boys give you a description?"

The Seattle police had not. They had never had any contact with James Worthington Jackson. They had looked him up in the telephone directory, found him listed, and called him to tell him, as requested, that his uncle was dead. They had got no answer. They had sent a car around to the address listed and found the closed shop, with the sign on the door. Shops nearby were closed. "It's Christmas there too, M.L." They had found one resident in a nearby house. He didn't know Jackson. He had never had need of electrical appliances. He didn't know if he'd have gone to that shop if he had. Looked like a hole in the wall to him. He did pass it every morning on his way to work. He had a vague feeling he had seen the sign on the door for a couple of weeks. Maybe not quite that long; maybe longer. He'd wondered, mildly, if it was ever going to be reopened. He'd never seen it doing much business.

They had found a woman in another house who had, some months before, taken a toaster in to be repaired. She hadn't noticed what Jackson looked like, but thought he was pretty young. Maybe in his twenties somewhere. She was in her late sixties, an age from which a good many people look pretty young. The toaster hadn't worked much better after he repaired it.

"They went to quite a lot of trouble for us, didn't they?" Heimrich said.

Forniss agreed the Seattle police had been diligent.

"The lab boys?"

A trooper had found a hole in the Heimrichs' ash tree by the terrace. He had dug into it and found a slug. Probably, by its weight, a .22 slug. Otherwise, an anonymous bullet. "Mashed up when it hit the tree. Never get anything out of it, the lab boys say. Looks like somebody drove a nail into that tree of yours, M.L. Years ago, and the bark grew over it. Bullet hit the nail, and that banged up the bullet. So—nothing to compare."

The lab boys had had better luck with the Pontiac station wagon. Partially better luck, at any rate. They had found a long scratch on the right rear fender, and red paint embedded in it. The paint was being analyzed.

"Probably from Miss Collins's Volks, M.L. Where the wagon brushed it forcing it off the road. They're running a comparison. Know by tomorrow, they think."

On the other hand, there was nothing on the rear bumper of the wagon, or anywhere on its rear end, to show that it had recently backed into anything.

"Like a man, M.L."

Heimrich had not really supposed there would be. Humans are not that solid. Sometimes bits of cloth, threads, adhere to a car which has struck a man. Not this time.

There had been a good many fingerprints and blurs of prints on the wagon. "Most of them Father Armstrong's, probably. They'll pick his up when they get a chance. Seems he's got services going on most of today."

Anglo-Catholics do have a good many services on Christmas Day.

"By the way," Forniss said, "they had to move that candlelight parade inside the church last night. Too windy out for candles."

Heimrich had supposed it would be—too windy and too cold.

"Oh," Forniss said, "and there weren't any prints at all on the ignition key."

"It's winter," Heimrich said. "People do wear gloves, Charlie."

Charles Forniss supposed so, although ignition keys are awkward in gloved fingers.

"So," Heimrich said, "you did get to see Bertram Friday?"

Forniss had seen Friday. Friday had still been cutting up the fallen tree. "Getting along pretty well with it," Forniss said. "Piling up a lot of firewood. Starting to split up the trunk lengths. The man's a good worker."

"And picking a damn cold day for it," Heimrich said. "Wonder who's going to burn it, don't you?"

"Probably this James Worthington," Forniss said. "Assuming he shows up. To learn what he's fallen heir to."

"Yes, Charlie. Seattle's a long way from here, isn't it. How long would it take to drive here from there, do you suppose?"

Forniss had no supposition to offer. It depended on how many miles a day somebody wanted to drive. He himself thought three hundred miles a day, or 350, was enough, especially with reasonable adherence to the fifty-five limit. But a lot of people thought nothing of five hundred, and some did even more. "Younger types," Forniss said, with some wistfulness in his voice. A week, maybe. Maybe twice that long. This time of year, a man might run into a lot of snow.

"Also," Forniss added, "we've got one wagon. We don't really need another."

Heimrich agreed. He also noted there was no special dearth of Pontiac station wagons and the fact that they had found a wagon which probably had forced a Volks off a road didn't necessarily mean that they had the one which had been used to kill a man.

Forniss said, "We-ell." Heimrich agreed. "But," he said, "something a defense attorney would be likely to point out, Charlie. To get back to Friday."

Bertram Friday had been reasonably cooperative and forthcoming. He thought Mr. Jackson had gone to the Lords' picnic on the Fourth of July. Anyway, Friday had made a big lobster salad for Mr. Jackson to take as a contribution to the food supply. Friday had put it in an ice chest in the car. He didn't know whether Jackson had taken along his movie camera. He thought probably he had. Last few months he had taken it almost everywhere. "A new toy for him," Friday had said. "He needed something to interest him, Lieutenant. He was—well, he was sort of a lonely man, since his wife died."

Jackson had not talked to him about the picnic. If he had taken movies at it, he had never run them for Friday.

Huh? No, he didn't own a rifle. Well, yes. Mr. Jackson did own one. It was probably around somewhere. He couldn't remember ever seeing Mr. Jackson use it.

Could he himself use a rifle?

"He froze up a little on that," Forniss said. "Wanted to know what I was getting at. Did I think he was the one who'd shot Mr. Lord? And why the hell would he? He'd never even seen the man. I told him we just checked up on things as we went along and that I wasn't accusing him of anything. Calmed him down. Not that he seemed stirred up, particularly. Just surprised, sort of. And, yes, he knew how to use a rifle. Hadn't for years, but he guessed he still could. Turns out, M.L., he did a hitch in the Corps. Made sergeant, he told me. And he dug up the rifle. In a storage closet it was. Winchester caliber thirty it is. Nice clean gun. Nothing to show it's been used recently."

"If it had been, there wouldn't be," Heimrich said, stating the obvious. "So the path, Charles?"

Of course Friday knew about the path along the ridge far above the Hudson—the path which ran north three or four miles from a beginning just beyond the end of N.Y. 109, and ran beyond the Jackson property, and the Heimrich property and the land owned by Oliver Larkin; the land from which somebody had fired a shot at two young people standing on the Heimrich terrace to watch the sun go down. Sure he knew it. Yes, he'd walked it a few times. If the Lieutenant wanted to look at it, he could go through a gap in the stone wall behind the house. Although it would be one hell of a cold day to walk it.

"I told him it was one hell of a cold day to be sawing wood," Forniss said, "and he agreed it sure was, but that he had to get it done because—he stopped with that, M.L."

"Because Mr. Jackson likes wood fires, I suppose. And doesn't like his front yard cluttered up with fallen trees. It's hard to switch over sometimes. To adjust. It was cold on the path, Charlie?"

It had been damn cold on the path, where the wind had its full sweep. Walking north, Forniss had walked against the wind. "Must have been blowing forty knots." He had walked fast to get it over with—as fast as the wind would let him walk. It had taken him eighteen minutes to reach the first gap in the dry stone fence of the Larkin property. Through the gap, it was not more than a hundred yards to the top of the knoll from which, presumably, somebody had fired a shot—a shot meant to silence Joan Collins. Again, presumably.

Two very cold troopers were pawing through tall grass looking for a cartridge case. Forniss had sent them there. When he appeared, he had been greeted with modified joy, on the assumption he had come to tell them to call it off.

"Knew there wasn't more than one chance in a million," Forniss said. "Hadn't been mowed since July, at a guess. Told them to give it another hour and check in at the barracks."

"Trampled down when they got there?"

"They couldn't see that it was, M.L. But they couldn't be sure it wasn't. Wind like this could have blown it straight again, I suppose."

He had left two cold men groping in tall grass for a tiny object which probably was not there and gone back along the path to the Jackson house and his car. This time he had jogged, with the wind behind him. Jogging, he needed only thirteen minutes.

"He could have done it easily," Forniss said. "Been back in time to be sawing wood when we showed up."

Heimrich nodded his head. He looked at his empty glass. After all, it was Christmas. He held the glass up for Joe Shepley to see. Shepley saw it and nodded. Forniss held his glass up. Shepley nodded his head again. When he brought the drinks, he also brought a menu. Roast turkey, of course. Also roast goose, cranberry sauce. For the unorthodox, even roast beef. Mashed potatoes or baked Idahoes. Choice of vegetables. Tossed green salad, with choice of dressing. Mince pie, pumpkin pie, or fruitcake with brandy sauce. Yes, he supposed the kitchen could manage a couple of beef sandwiches, although the complete dinner was all they were supposed to be serving. He'd have the waitress ask.

"Suppose, after we eat," Heimrich said, "you try to get Seattle on the phone, Charlie. You know anybody there?"

To Heimrich's surprise, Forniss shook his head. So there was one place in the world Charlie Forniss didn't know anybody. Well, nobody's perfect. Heimrich was still a little surprised.

"Ask them to try and find out when he closed up his shop," Heimrich said. "Somebody ought to know. And what he looks like. Somebody ought to have seen him. Tall or short? Does he still wear his hair long? Did he have his wagon tuned up recently, like for a long trip? Anything they can dig up about him. O.K.?"

"O.K., M.L. And you?"

"I'm going home," Heimrich said. "After all, it's Christmas. And after you talk to Seattle, go home yourself, huh? Oh, you might set it up for us to use a projector in the morning. We may as well have a look at Sam Jackson's movie. Could be he took a picture of a murderer."

Forniss said, "Yeah. Be convenient if he did, wouldn't it?"

The kitchen had condescended to supply roast beef sandwiches. The beef was overdone.

Chapter 12

THEY HAD FINISHED DINNER and were in front of the fire when the telephone rang. Merton Heimrich was having cognac with his coffee. The others had declined, Joan and Michael without comment; Susan with the reflection that they had, after all, had wine with dinner and that she was afraid the turkey had been a little dried out. "At best," she said, "turkey is an overrated bird. Next Christmas, I'm going to try and find a goose." She was told that, to everybody else, the turkey had seemed perfect.

"Everything was," Joan Collins said. "If things hadn't happened, I'd have been taken to a restaurant for dinner. Someplace where everybody knows Father. Probably a French restaurant in the East Fifties. One that everybody's going to at the moment. Everybody like Father, that is. I'm sorry. Maybe I shouldn't have had that second glass of wine. All right, perhaps I don't feel the way I ought to about my father."

"There's no way anybody *ought* to feel about anybody," Susan told her. "There's just the way people do."

It was then the telephone rang. Joan had lifted her coffee cup and it jumped in her hand. A little coffee sloshed into the saucer. Michael put a hand, gently, on her knee. She smiled at him. She said, "I'm all right, Michael. I'm just the sort that jumps when there's a noise I'm not expecting." Michael said, "Sure, baby," but he did not, immediately, take the reassuring pressure from her knee.

Susan did not make a point of not seeing or hearing any of this.

Across the room, Heimrich said his name into the telephone. Then he said, "Yes, Charlie. Thought I told you to call it— All right, you remembered you did maybe know a guy who might be on the Seattle force. So?"

So the man Forniss remembered—a former Naval intelligence officer—was a detective captain on the Seattle police force. He had expedited matters.

James Worthington Jackson had showed up about four that afternoon, Seattle time. He had come by taxi, not by Pontiac station wagon. His arrival had happened to coincide with that of Detective Brian O'Halloran. O'Halloran had told Jackson of his uncle's death. Jackson had seemed appropriately shocked and, initially, unbelieving. He had said, "Not the dear old guy. Hell, I thought he'd live forever."

He himself had just got fed up with sitting around a shop to which nobody much came. Well, about two weeks ago. All right, he had closed up the shop in the middle of the gift-buying season. "Thing is, I'd pretty well sold out and a shipment I had coming didn't show up. So I didn't have much of anything to sell."

With nothing much to sell, and not many buyers anyway, Jackson had decided "to take myself a little vacation." He had driven up into the mountains to a ski lodge. "Dinky little place, but one I could run to."

"Seems a very confiding sort," Heimrich commented. Forniss agreed James Worthington Jackson seemed to be a forthcoming man. "Drove up in his station wagon," Heimrich said. "Came back by bus and taxi?"

"Yeah. What he told this O'Halloran."

"Somebody repossess the Pontiac?"

"Way he tells it, the car conked out and he left it to be repaired. Doesn't remember offhand the name of the garage he left it at, but he can find it again. Thinks it was in a town named Lone Wolf. Or maybe Wolf Run. But he can find it."

"Being checked out," the teletype reported. "Will advise."

"Very cooperative people in Seattle," Heimrich said. "Lucky it turned out you did know somebody on the force, probably. So?"

So Jackson had taken a bus back to Seattle, and a cab from the bus terminal. And he had planned to get a friend to drive him up to get the Pontiac. Early next week, they'd told him it would be ready. The garage was having to send away for parts.

But now Jackson didn't know. Did O'Halloran know about the funeral arrangements for his uncle? O'Halloran didn't.

Neither did Heimrich. The body, possibly by now, certainly by tomorrow, would be at the local undertaker's. (Who called himself a "mortician" and his place of business a "funeral parlor." It was known locally as "Marty's Layaway.") "We'll call him tomorrow," Heimrich said. "Soon as we know. Suit his convenience, of course, if he's flying East. They get a description of him, Charlie?"

"Sort of. About five eight, they say. Doesn't weigh more than a hundred twenty, is O'Halloran's guess. Hippie type, O'Halloran says. Apparently because he's got long hair."

Heimrich said, "Mmm." Forniss said, "Yeah. There are airplanes, of course. But the cab picked him up at the bus terminal."

"Tomorrow we'll have to do some checking," Heimrich said. "The lab boys come up with anything more?"

The scrapings of red paint from the right rear fender of the station wagon they had were chemically identical with those taken from Joan Collins's Volks. The serial number of the Pontiac had been forwarded to the New York Motor Vehicle Bureau, which was closed for Christmas. They would determine whether the Pontiac was Father Armstrong's. The slug dug out of the Heimrichs' ash tree wasn't going to be of any help. Nothing to compare with anything. The two cold troopers on the Larkins knoll hadn't found a cartridge case and had, as directed, knocked off. Forniss would put more men on it tomorrow, if Heimrich wanted. He doubted if a cartridge case would come of it.

"We'll see tomorrow," Heimrich said. "Meanwhile you call it a day, Charlie. I have, far's I know, anyway."

Policemen can see no further into the future than civilians. On the whole, they probably can see less far. Michael had brought blankets out for his sofa-bed, as what Heimrich suspected was a symbol of conformity to the prejudices of ancients, when the doorbell rang. "Who on earth at this hour?" Susan said, and Heimrich went to find out, looking at his watch as he crossed to the door. It was ten minutes after eleven, certainly an odd hour for a drop-in caller.

The doorbell had been rung by a slim youth, slim despite a heavy short coat. His regular-featured face looked a little pinched with cold. He wore a knitted wool cap which came down over his ears. He said, "Sorry, sir. I'm looking for Inspector Heimrich of the state police."

Heimrich said, "Yes? Well, you've found him. You'd better come on in out of the cold, I guess."

The youth came in. He took off the stocking cap and loosened his coat. His blond hair, with the cap off, was short, was almost a crew cut.

"I know it's too late to be bothering—" he said, and stopped in midsentence. He said, "Hi, Mike. I didn't know you'd come down."

Nobody who knows him well calls Michael Faye "Mike." Michael looked, slowly, at the slim youth.

"I don't know that I—" Michael said, and the slim blond youth shook his head and smiled.

"Tennis last summer," he said. "You were too good for us. Miles too good. I'm Alan Lord. No reason you should remember me, I guess. Just another lousy tennis player. At our court. Last June it was. None of us belonged on the same court with——"

"Sure I remember," Michael said. "Hi, Alan."

Michael's not much of a liar, Heimrich thought. He didn't know this boy from—well, from Adam. Except, now, as a bunny tennis player. So this is Alan Lord, adopted son of Burton Lord, deceased.

"May as well take your coat off, Mr. Lord," Heimrich said. The boy was probably about Michael's age, and so rated the "Mr." "This is Mrs. Heimrich. And Miss Collins. You wanted to see me about something?"

"Yes, I did, sir. But—well, I guess I thought you'd be more like

the others. Like that man Cochran, I guess. He—well, he badgered
my mother. Oh, good evening, Mrs. Heimrich, Miss Collins. Sorry
I barged in on you like this. I—I just happened to be going by on
my way home and I thought—" He stopped. After a moment he
said, "I guess it wasn't such a good idea, maybe."

"All right, son," Heimrich said. "What was the idea? To tell me
to quit badgering your mother? I didn't badger her. The District
Attorney asked me to check with her before Mrs. Kemper goes on
trial. I explained that to her. Does she say I badgered her, Mr.
Lord?"

"No, sir. She didn't put it that way. It's just—well, she's been
through enough, hasn't she? His getting shot by this—this whore of
his. I'm sorry, ma'am. I shouldn't have put it that way. But it's the
way it was."

"I've heard the word," Susan said. "So has Miss Collins, I imagine." She looked at Merton Heimrich, who towered above the
slight young man. "You'd really better take your coat off, Mr.
Lord. It's warm in here."

Lord took off his heavy short coat. Under it he was wearing a
dark gray business suit, and a white shirt and a dark blue necktie.
Dressy for the country, she thought. Perhaps, of course, he had
spent the evening in the city and was on his way home. If so, he
had left the mother about whom he was so concerned alone on
Christmas Day.

"You stopped by to ask me to lay off your mother," Heimrich
said. "Not—well, not to be rough on her, as I gather you think Detective Cochran was. You didn't need to, Mr. Lord. I think your
mother will agree with that. And Mrs. Kemper isn't a whore. She
and your father were having an affair. She doesn't deny that."

"Not father, sir. Stepfather. My real father is George Nolan, Inspector. You've probably heard of him. Most people have, I guess.
He's quite well known, sir. I'm Alan Nolan, really. Ought to be,
anyhow."

"Yes," Heimrich said. "I've heard of your father. As you say,
he's very well known. So was your stepfather, come to that."

Alan Lord had no immediate comment. After almost a minute,

he said, "I suppose so, sir. In a different sort of way, though. Dad is —I guess you'd have to call him an intellectual, wouldn't you?"

Heimrich felt no such compulsion. He let it ride.

"I mean," Alan said, "Mr. Lord put on a lot of plays. Not very good plays. I'd think. Old-fashioned comedies and things like that, you know. Not—well, not really with it, if you know what I mean."

Heimrich supposed he did. Plays, the boy probably meant, which had been approved by members of an antique generation; tottering oldsters like—well, like Inspector Merton Heimrich. But all Heimrich said was, "A good many people seem to have liked them, son."

"Oh," Lord said, "my stepfather made a lot of money out of them, all right." His emphasis put the word "money" between quotation marks. It was rather as if he spoke of offal. "Dad was blacklisted once. Somebody—McCarthy, I think it was—said he was a Communist. He wasn't, of course. But a lot of papers dropped his column."

The evil that men do lives after them, Heimrich thought. Not very vividly in this young mind, seemingly. Also, it was getting late.

"I'm sorry if you think I badgered your mother, Mr. Lord. I didn't. Just wanted to get things straight for District Attorney Peters. About your stepfather's murder. You weren't at the picnic when it happened, your mother tells me."

"No, sir. We were running out of ice and Mother asked me to go get some. Anyway, he was making that speech of his, so it was all right with me."

"Yes," Heimrich said. "And your mother was in the kitchen, conferring with the caterers. So neither of you saw Mr. Lord killed. That's the way it was?"

"Yes. But there wasn't anything we could have done about it, Inspector. Nothing anybody could have done about it. She was in the next field when she shot at him. A hundred yards away, maybe. What they tell me, anyway."

"Pretty good shooting," Heimrich said. "Wouldn't you say so, Mr. Lord?"

"I guess so, sir. She was a member of the rifle team at the club. I guess she was pretty good. Some of us aren't too bad, you know."

"Us, Mr. Lord?"

"Of them was what I meant to say, Inspector. Turned out I wasn't any good at it. Couldn't hit the side of a barn, as people used to say. No better with a rifle than I am with a racket, and Mike can tell you how bad that is."

Michael didn't say anything, which, of course, was a way of saying something.

"Guess I'm just an iceman," Lord said. "Way my stepfather thought of me, anyway."

Heimrich smiled indulgently, the smile accepting and discounting an obvious libel.

"I doubt if he did," Heimrich said. "Anyway, icemen are useful. Were in my early days, anyway. And you did get ice for the picnic, didn't you?"

Young Lord grinned at that. He nodded his head. Then he said, "Yeah. And as a matter of fact, it wasn't all that easy. I had to go three places. Tony, he's the guy runs the Gulf station, had run out. So had the Sunoco station down the road. Had to go clear down to the shopping center to find a machine that still had ice in it. And I got the last two bags. I was supposed to get at least four. Decided to take what I could get, before people had to drink warm drinks. Two was plenty, way things turned out."

Which, Heimrich thought, was one way of putting it. That the picnic had collapsed when its host had been murdered was another. There hadn't, by the time Alan Lord had got back, been much demand for ice.

"All right, Mr. Lord. Probably I won't have to bother your mother again."

"Look," the slim boy said, "I'm the one doing the bothering. It was a fool idea, anyway."

He reached for his coat and began to shrug into it. "Ought to have had better sense," he said. He took a step or two toward the door. He stopped and turned. "Hope all of you will forgive me," he said. "Good night, sir—Mrs. Heimrich, Miss Collins. Probably be seeing you around, Mike."

Michael Faye said, "Sure."

Heimrich went to the door with him, and Lord fitted the stocking cap on his head and went out to his car. His car, Heimrich noted, was a Mercedes sports model. Young Lord could afford to put quotation marks around the word "money."

Heimrich went back to the fire, welcome now after the cold blast through the opened door.

"You didn't recognize him when he first came in, did you?" he said to Michael.

"Not at first, Dad. Last summer he was wearing his hair long. Down pretty near to his shoulders. Had to put a strap around it when he was playing tennis. But I told you that, didn't I? And that he was a bit of a weirdo."

"Yes, Michael," Heimrich said. "You did tell me that."

As he undressed for bed, after making sure lights were off and doors locked and saying good night to Michael on his sofa, Heimrich wondered why his stepson thought of Alan Lord as a "weirdo." A well-brought-up, polite young man, he had seemed to Merton Heimrich. Perhaps a little given to "sirs": undoubtedly a little impulsive. Not, it seemed, too deeply grieved by his stepfather's death. As Susan had pointed out, there is no "ought" about affection. Joan Collins's affection for her "real" father was, apparently, minimal. Her affection for Michael Faye was, almost as evidently, not.

Kids are funny, he thought, hanging his shirt over the back of a chair. Michael is funny about his emphasis on the sofa, his ostentatious lugging out of blankets. Kids make assumptions about their elders: parents, particularly, have forgotten the bright joy of sex, if, indeed, they ever knew it. Well, probably he had felt the same way about his own parents.

Susan was already in her bed, but her eyes were open. Her eyes said "Yes . . ."

The sun was bright the next morning. The wind had died down. The window thermometer said six below zero. The frigid Buick, resentful of a night in an unheated garage, declined for a long time to take any part in the proceedings. The starter ground for minutes before getting even a reluctant cough. Finally, the engine caught. When he put the gear lever at "R" the engine stopped again, with what appeared to be finality. Not in this weather, the Buick said. It took a lot of grinding to make it change its mind. Fortunately, the battery stayed alive and vigorous.

Backed out of the garage and turned toward the drive, the Buick didn't want to go forward, either. It was, however, a little easier to cajole. The little evergreen by the drive hadn't made it. It was lying flat, its slender trunk broken. It was still matted with ice.

What with one thing and another, including Susan's insistence that two cups of coffee were inadequate as a breakfast on an icy day, Heimrich was almost half an hour late at his office in the headquarters building of Troop K. Forniss wasn't in yet; he had, after all, been at it until almost midnight. The lab had found nothing that would prove, or disprove, that the Pontiac station wagon had backed into a man and killed him. That it had sideswiped a red Volks was another matter. Paint analysis had proved that to the satisfaction of the lab. Nobody, of course, could tell about a jury. And it might have grazed another red Volks.

The tire chains on the Pontiac were as worn as was to be expected considering Father Armstrong's habit of having them put on in late fall and removed the following spring, come snow or no snow. The chain on the left rear was, in fact, lacking a crossbar. It was a wonder the chain had stayed on the tire. The salvage crew—two troopers—had had to take the chains off before they could drive the wagon to the barracks. This had meant jacking the car up on soft ground and climbing under it. It had been a nasty job, but neither of the troopers had been killed doing it.

The rifle slug from the ash tree was not going to be of use to anybody. Banged up beyond the powers of any comparison microscope to untangle. And they had no rifle to compare it with, assuming comparison had been possible. The only rifle concerned was locked up at the county seat, waiting to be entered as Exhibit A in the trial of the People of the State of New York v. Loren Kemper. Oh, the slug probably was from a .22 caliber rifle like the alleged murder weapon in Carmel.

There were papers in Heimrich's In basket. They included last night's teletype from Seattle. It was what Forniss had said it was.

There wouldn't be anything further from Seattle until, at best, afternoon. It was still—what? Half-past six in the morning in Seattle. Three hours' difference in time. Enough to make it possible for someone to force a Volks off the road at about eight thirty in the morning and make it to the Newark airport and show up in Seattle about four in the afternoon? Heimrich doubted it, but it could be checked out. Probably Charlie Forniss had already checked it. No, certainly not time enough to ditch a Pontiac station wagon off the driveway to Sam Jackson's house and then get on to Newark. In what? Another wagon, which had brushed another red car? A matter of coincidence? A possibility which could be rejected, if not quite out of hand. The most outrageous coincidences are still conceivable, if to policemen unwelcome. A million-to-one chance, but still a chance. Charlie to check flight schedules to the West Coast, when he got in.

Meanwhile—

Meanwhile, Heimrich's telephone rang. He said "Yes?" to it. District Attorney Jonathan Peters was calling. Would Inspector Heimrich hold on a minute? People with secretaries always expect other people to hold on a minute.

It was more than a minute. Then it was, "Peters here. Who's this?"

"Heimrich. You called me, Mr. Peters."

"Huh? Oh, yeah. They tell me you were up here yesterday. Poking around, apparently. Seeing this Kemper woman. That right, Inspector?"

"I saw Mrs. Kemper, yes."

"What the hell about? Nothing for you people to be messing in, way I see it."

District Attorney Peters was going to be difficult. Heimrich had expected he would be.

"About a probable murder in Van Brunt, Mr. Peters. Which is, as you know, an unincorporated village." The state police do not operate in incorporated communities unless requested to. "And the Lord place is beyond the Cold Harbor limits."

He had not needed to add the last. He finds Jonathan Peters somewhat annoying. He had for years.

If his comment had irritated Peters, Peters decided to lay irritation aside. For the moment, anyway.

"What do you mean probable murder, Heimrich? You talking about that hit-and-run?"

"Intentional hit-and-run, Mr. Peters. The way it looks to us. Hence, murder, Mr. Peters. The victim, Samuel Jackson, Mrs. Kemper's attorney. So, I went to ask Mrs. Kemper about him. Matter of routine, you know."

"The hell I do. But I can't stop your nosing around, I suppose. Damn nuisance, all the same. So is Jackson's getting himself killed, come to that."

"Yes?"

"She'll get a new lawyer. If she can find somebody damn fool enough to take her case on. And he'll move for a postponement and the judge—Peabody it'll be—will have to grant it, under the circumstances. And that will louse up our operations. It's a damn nuisance, Heimrich."

Merton Heimrich could see it might be. Due process of law now and then disconcerts some district attorneys who want to get on with their job, which, to many, is to put people in prison and thus to please voters. Peters was that kind of district attorney.

"It's not as if she's got a prayer," Peters said. "Hell, man, I saw it happen. Saw her shoot old Burton. Swear myself in and testify to that. Can't see why a man like Jackson would take her on. Except he didn't know much about criminal practice, I understand. Maybe they were sleeping together. That might explain it. Wouldn't put it past her, would you?"

"I only met her yesterday, Mr. Peters. She didn't impress me as a woman who sleeps around. But I could be wrong, of course. I did know Sam Jackson. I doubt if he did much sleeping around. He was—well, a bit old for it."

"You never can tell, Heimrich. You ought to know that. Anyway, she was sleeping with Lord. And he breaks it off. Just like that. So, she killed him while he was making a speech at this picnic. I was there and saw her do it. I keep telling you that."

"I know you do, Mr. Peters. I don't question it. County case, after all. She was a hundred yards or so away, as I get it. But it was a bright, hot afternoon, I understand."

"And I've got twenty-twenty vision, Heimrich."

Heimrich was sure he had. "And probably," he said, "there were other people who saw her too. Pretty open about it, she was, apparently. In full sight of maybe seventy-five, a hundred, people."

"Mostly, people were looking at Burton. Or at each other. But sure, I've got other witnesses who saw her with the rifle. And she admits it was her rifle. Damn good piece, the rifle is. And she was good with it. Belonged to this rifle team at the country club, and they all say she was tops. Funny thing for a woman to take up, wouldn't you say? Unless she was getting in practice in case Lord walked out on her. See what I mean?"

Heimrich agreed it was an interesting theory. If not, he thought, a very plausible one. He didn't suppose Peters did either. But you could never be entirely sure about the Honorable Jonathan Peters, District Attorney, Putnam County, New York. Peters had once got an armed robbery case, which Heimrich had prepared, thrown out of court by asking questions a second-year law student should have known would lead to a mistrial.

"What I called you about," Peters said, "I don't want you boys messing around with the Lord case. You understand that, Inspector?"

"Perfectly," Heimrich said. "No reason we should, Mr. Peters. Unless there's a tie-in with something else we're working on. Like the murder of Mr. Jackson."

"What you say was a murder, Inspector. What probably was an ordinary hit-and-run. Anyway, what would be the tie-in? So Jackson was the Kemper woman's lawyer. So what?"

"I don't know what, Mr. Peters. Could be you're right. If you are, we'll lay off."

"See that you do," Peters said, and hung up.

He's not an easy man to get along with, Heimrich thought. Could be, I suppose, I'm not either. I wonder if he *has* got twenty-twenty vision. I wonder if last Fourth of July *was* a bright, clear day. A hot one, from what people say. Sometimes there's a heat haze on hot summer afternoons. I'll have to ask Charlie about that when he gets in, which ought to be any time now, even if he did work until near midnight.

Heimrich ignored the considerable amount of material in his In basket. He leaned back in his chair, closed his eyes, and thought about a Pontiac station wagon. Late on the evening of one day it had been backed into a man and killed him. The next morning, around eight thirty, it looked like, it had forced a red Volkswagen off the road, turning the Volks partway over and endangering the Volks occupant. Where had the station wagon spent the night?

In the stub road off Jackson's driveway? If Friday had driven it, that was a possibility. But why would he have used the wagon for either of the purposes it had been used for? Killed Jackson for fifty thousand dollars? Possibly, of course. Tried to kill Joan Collins because of what she might have seen from her second-floor window at the inn? Again, possibly. And walked or jogged along a path, facing a brutal wind and carrying his employer's rifle, to have another try at murder? Oh, just conceivably.

Then, no connection at all with the planned murder of Burton Lord, semiretired theatrical producer. Which would leave Peters right. No reason apparent why Friday should have killed Lord; a possible reason why Loren Kemper might have. Woman scorned, woman rejected, woman enraged to the point of murder. A motive that appealed to Jonathan Peters, and might to a jury. Why doesn't it appeal to me? Merton Heimrich wondered. It's the sort of thing that does happen. But, to the young, the violent young, frantic with hurt pride; convulsively in love. Doubt merely because Loren Kemper doesn't seem the type? Come off it, Heimrich. Murderers do not come by type. Neither do lovers.

Get back to the station wagon. Parked overnight in a place convenient for Bertram Friday? Concealed, but not effectively concealed. Having been forced that far up the stub road, it could have been jammed farther, into the open field Sam Jackson had once used as a parking lot for guests. Concealed, or meant to be found? In an out-of-the-way place, certainly, for anyone except Friday. Rammed in among the bushes by somebody who then walked away? Toward home, or toward a preparked car?

Speculation, in the absence of facts, doesn't often get a cop anywhere. Oh, Sherlock Holmes. But Holmes wasn't a cop, and facts didn't always bother him much. He had believed, or asked readers to believe, that a snake could climb up, shinny up, a loosely dangling rope.

"Morning, Charlie." Heimrich had opened his eyes at the sound of his office door opening.

Lieutenant Charles Forniss didn't look like a man who had been up working most of the night.

He said, "Morning, M.L. I checked the airport. No soap."

"Newark?"

"Westchester County, M.L. Only way he could have done it. No record of a charter flight from Westchester to Newark. No Pontiac station wagon parked at Westchester. Oh, I checked Newark, too. No plane out of there would have got him to Seattle at the time he showed up there. Kennedy, maybe. Newark to Kennedy by the chopper. Just possible, maybe. Got Sergeant Lacey checking. But I doubt it like hell."

"So do I," Heimrich said. "I'm afraid young Jackson was a continent away. You went over to Lord's place the day he was killed, interrupted while making his Fourth of July picnic speech. What kind of day was it, Charlie? Hot, I understand?"

"Hot as hell. Upper nineties, at a guess."

"Clear, sunny day?"

"Clear, all right. But sort of hazy, way I remember it. Way it gets in the afternoon sometimes in summer."

"Suppose," Heimrich said, "we go look at some movies, Charlie."

Chapter 13

It was a very small movie theater they went to—an office blacked out for the occasion. The state police do not spend much time looking at home movies. They do not often have the time to waste, as he and Forniss were wasting theirs now, Heimrich thought. He said, "Roll it, Spender," to the trooper who had already threaded Sam Jackson's film into a projector. Spender was one of the police photographers.

A picture came up on the small screen. It was in black and white —well, in dark gray and lighter gray. It was a head-on view of a raccoon, eating from a bird feeder. The raccoon was very brisk about it. He picked morsels of food from the feeder with small quick hands. Now and then he paused and looked at the camera. He had an alert small face.

"Cute little bastards," Forniss said.

The raccoon peered into the feeder and then used one small hand to make sure. Then he backed down the tree and went off along the ground, the camera following him. Seen from the rear, the raccoon was no longer cute. His rear end didn't match his front end. His rear was heavy and he waddled as he walked. Going away, he was heavy and slow.

"Robs too many bird feeders," Forniss commented. "Or turns over too many garbage cans."

The retreating coon vanished. For a moment, the screen merely flickered. Then it produced a woodchuck, sitting on his haunches, small forepaws dangling. He looked expectant, like a hopeful beggar. His appearance was brief. He was followed by a squirrel, rather blurred and apparently in flight.

"Looks as if he got a red," Forniss said. "From the size of it. Pretty blurry, though."

"Too fast for the camera," Spender said. "Also out of focus. Pretty hipped on animals, whoever took this was. Naturalist or something?"

Nobody answered him because pictures flickered on the screen again. This time the animals were human. There were two men, both in shorts and sports shirts and two women, one in shorts and the other in slacks. All four were drinking.

"Peters, it could be," Forniss said. "The one at the end. Could be the fat one in pants is his wife. A picnic, anyway. Let's hope it's the right—"

The camera had panned away from the four. It swept a wide grassy area, with other groups, some with plates, more with lifted glasses, some sitting on the grass, others in director's chairs and deck chairs. The faces of most of them were a little blurred.

"Whole damned thing's out of focus," Spender said. "Guy must have been an amateur. Maybe just learning."

"It's the right picnic, M.L.," Forniss said. "There's Lord himself."

The camera had ceased its searching. The picture now was of a somewhat heavy man, in what appeared to be a white tennis shirt and white slacks. He was standing on a low wooden platform and, obviously, he was speaking. Now and then he gestured. Once he appeared to laugh.

"Finally got something in focus," Spender said.

The pictured speaker held both hands out in front of him, in what appeared to be a welcoming gesture. He was smiling. He had thick white hair, smoothly barbered.

Then he fell forward, off the platform. Almost at once people were running toward him, blocking the fallen man from the camera. The picture lifted above them and focused—almost focused—

on a low stone wall. It was there only a second. Then it was a picture of a field. It was a blur at first; then it grew in definition. It was a picture of a bending figure, which appeared to be rubbing something on the ground.

Hair streamed down over the face of the bending person, screening the face from the camera.

"I'll be goddamned," Forniss said. "I'll be damned to hell."

"Yes," Heimrich said. "Picture of a murderer, Charlie. And—"

He stopped, because the person in the picture had straightened up. It began to run, apparently up a slope. The camera tried to follow it, but it ran out of the camera's range. Vaguely, beyond the running figure there was a shape, which appeared to be that of a house.

The picture disappeared from the screen. There was only white light on the screen.

"All we've got," Spender said. "Film ran out there."

"Nothing that helps much, is there?" Forniss said. "Can't see the face. And a lot of people saw her rub the rifle in the grass to get rid of the prints."

"Yes," Heimrich said. "Saw somebody, anyway. Somebody going off up a slope at a dead run. After rubbing something in the grass. Damp grass, probably, if it was a humid day. Hazy day. Peters must have seen more than we did, wouldn't you say, Charlie? Seen a face, or thought he did. No, I can't see we're helped much. But Sam Jackson filed it under 'E,' didn't he? 'E' for 'evidence,' you think, Charlie? Let's run the last part again, Spender."

Spender ran the picnic scenes again. They didn't seem much clearer.

"Could have been foggy, way it looks," Spender said. "In addition to lack of focus."

Heimrich said "Mmm" in an abstracted way and again the film ran out.

"Once more," Heimrich said. "And watch the running, Charlie. See if you notice anything about it."

Spender ran the picnic scenes again, and the running figure

again. And Charlie Forniss said, "Well, I *will* be damned, M.L. Missed it the first time."

"So did I," Heimrich said. "Just—oh, felt there was something a little off. Women don't run like men, do they? Particularly looked at from behind. They're not put together the way we are. Legs attached differently. Something about the pelvis, I suppose."

"Yeah," Forniss said. "We don't need the room for babies. Long-haired man, it could have been. I still don't see how he managed it, do you? Have to be in two places at the same time, pretty much. Here and Seattle, unless he had some dodge we haven't—"

He stopped, because Heimrich was, slowly, shaking his head.

"No," Heimrich said. "I don't think we have to look as far away as Seattle. Among other things, no hookup I can see. I think we'd better check with the iceman, Charlie. Ice company, I mean."

"Ice company?" Forniss said. "Afraid I don't get it, M.L."

Heimrich filled Forniss in so he did get it.

"Yeah," Forniss said. "Six months ago, but we can give it a try. Crystal Clear Ice Corporation, I think they call it. Something like that, anyway."

Heimrich wouldn't put it past them.

"May take a while," Forniss said. "I'll get on it." He went out to get on it.

Heimrich leaned back in his desk chair and closed his eyes. So that was what Sam Jackson had had; what had made him volunteer to defend Loren Kemper. Something, obviously. But enough? A running figure in a dim photograph. Admissible as evidence? Probably. Exhibit A for the defense. Still, enough? Sam had not been a trial lawyer, but he had been an intelligent man, a shrewd man. He would have wanted more; wanted confirmation for a jury.

Expert confirmation. Which would have meant?

Heimrich leaned forward in his chair. He looked up a number in the telephone directory and dialed it.

Dr. Ernest Chandler was with a patient. He would be told Inspector Heimrich had called and would be asked—

"This is rather urgent," Heimrich said. "And it won't take more than a minute. So, unless he's operating on somebody——"

"Doctor seldom does surgery, Inspector. He's a general practitioner. Patients in need of surgery, he refers to a surgeon like——"

"I know," Heimrich said. "Get through to him, will you? Tell him I'll only need a minute or two. And tell him it's police business. O.K.?"

"We-ell, he doesn't like to be disturbed. You did say Inspector Heimrich?"

Heimrich had. Well, if he would hold on a minute?

He held on. Actually, it was more than a minute; it was almost four minutes. Then it was, "Dr. Chandler. Who is this?"

"Heimrich, Erni." (Dr. Ernest Chandler does not like his nickname. Merton Heimrich, who does not like any part of his given name, does not, especially, like to be kept waiting four minutes.)

"The girl's all right, isn't she? The one who ran her car off the road? Only minor bruises, far as I could tell. Sometimes they hold back on you."

"Miss Collins is all right, Doctor. I wanted to ask you something about Sam Jackson."

"Great old guy, Sam was. Damn shame what happened. But he's dead, M.L. Multiple head injuries. Must have died almost at once. And I'm not the coroner, you know."

"Listen a minute, Doctor. I know Sam's dead. Sometime before he was killed—sometime in the last few weeks, probably—did he come to you and ask you to recommend an orthopedic surgeon? Give him the name of one, that is?"

"Now how did you come up with that, M.L.?"

"Guessed, Ernest. Did I guess right?"

"Matter of fact, you did. He wanted the name of a good bone man, and I gave him one. Got it out of the registry. Don't know him myself. Belongs to all the right surgical societies. Dr. Theodore Dent. Graduated Columbia School of Medicine. Interned Johns Hopkins. Qualified as an orthopedist there. Passed his boards in Maryland, I think. Practices in White Plains. Something the matter with your bones, M.L.?"

"Not that I know of, Ernest. Sorry to have had to bother you."

"Come to think of it, you're about due for a checkup. Liz will make an appointment now for you, if you want."

"I'll call Miss Shepard back about that, Doctor. Dr. Theodore Dent in White Plains. That right?"

That was right.

It took longer to get Dr. Dent on the telephone. Dr. Dent was not in his office. He was at the hospital. Dr. Dent was in surgery and could not be disturbed. No, wait a minute. There he was now. "Dr. Dent. Dr. Theodore Dent. A call for you, Doctor." (This had the hollow clatter of a public address.) "I've paged him, Inspector. Here—yes, Doctor. An Inspector Heimrich."

The voice on the phone was light and clear. The enunciation was crisp.

"Dent here. *Inspector* Heimrich? What do you inspect, Inspector?"

"Crime, Doctor. State police."

"Haven't committed any lately, Inspector. Just sawed off a man's leg. Entirely legal. Signed permission from patient. Also, necessary amputation. Bone cancer. Maybe caught it in time. Can hope so, anyway. So?"

"So," Heimrich said, "a while back, maybe several weeks back, did a lawyer come to see you? A Samuel Jackson, from Van Brunt? Show you a film and ask you something about it?"

"Could be. Why don't you ask him about it, Inspector?"

"Because he's dead, Doctor. Probably murdered. Perhaps, indirectly, because of the picture he showed you. A picture of somebody running in a field."

"Too bad. Seemed a pleasant sort of man. Yes, he did ask me about the picture. Pretty fuzzy picture. Was the runner male or female?"

"And?"

"Male, obviously. Any intern could have told him that. Any layman with the faintest knowledge of anatomy. Put together differently, men and women are. Pelvic difference. Women wobble. Some more than others, of course. Depends on the weight somewhat. But all a little. Even women athletes. Runners. Way they're made. As somebody said, *vive la différence.*"

"Yes," Heimrich said. "Did Mr. Jackson ask you to testify to that, Doctor? That the person running was a male? Testify in court as an expert?"

"Asked me if I would, yes. If it came to that, he said. Told him I'd answer a subpoena if I had to. And that it would probably be damned inconvenient. Something about identity in a murder trial, I gathered."

"You will testify, Doctor? If it comes to that? And have no doubt about your opinion?"

"No room for doubt, Inspector. No possible room for doubt. Simply a fact. The running person was a male. Yes, I'll testify if I have to. But I'm a busy man, Inspector. Not too many bone men around here. Qualified ones, I mean."

"You may not have to, Doctor. Things are a little up in the air, with Sam Jackson dead. But somebody may be in touch with you."

"I hope not, but all right. Anything else, Inspector? Because I've got a couple of feet to do. Man fell off a roof and landed on concrete. Right side up. Preparing him now, they are."

"Nothing else, Doctor. And thanks."

Dr. Theodore Dent said, "O.K.," and hung up.

Merton Heimrich leaned back in his chair and closed his eyes again. No identification established, but one placed in doubt. Jonathan Peters wouldn't be happy about that.

Had Sam got more? Enough to make his death necessary for someone? Or had he merely guessed? After all, his purpose was only to get a client off, not to get somebody else on. The last was a job for the police—the New York State Police and, specifically, Inspector M. L. Heimrich and Lieutenant Charles Forniss. And what was keeping Charlie? Was the iceman freezing up on him?

He opened his eyes and said, "Yes, Charlie?" and Forniss came into the room and pulled a chair up in front of Heimrich.

"This Crystal Clear Ice Corporation," Forniss said. "Sizable company it turns out to be. Offices and plant in White Plains. Got its vending machines all over Westchester and Putnam counties. Even some over in Jersey. Yeah, they keep records. Took a while to look them up, but they're not very busy now. Slack season, with the weather what it is."

Heimrich said, "Naturally." Even Susan would admit that, this time, the word fitted.

"Last Fourth of July, they were busy as hell. The way they work it—"

The way they worked it was that they rented space for the ice vending machines. In shopping centers they rented space, like any other merchant. At gas stations, it was often on a commission basis, the station owner getting a percentage of the take. Heimrich, of course, knew how the machines worked. There was a slot for coins —quarters, preferably, but nickels and dimes accepted. No pennies. The customer poked coins in the slot. Fifty cents a bag. "Twice what it was a few years back, as what isn't?" Properly fed, the vending machine groaned and gurgled and, with a thump, laid an egg, its egg being a heavy, insulated bag of ice cubes.

The customer opened a compartment in the base of the machine, which the coins had unlocked, took out his bag, took it home, and iced his drinks.

The vending machines were numbered. The one at the Gulf station between the Lord place and Cold Harbor was G-1905. It had been filled from the truck at around eight o'clock on the morning of the Fourth of July. The money accumulated from the previous day's sales had been removed.

Since the day was hot, and the Fourth of July, G-1905 had been checked again in the early afternoon. "Probably about one thirty, they think." Twenty-five new bags had been added, and the deposited coins removed.

The Sunoco station farther down the road had also been checked twice. It had only needed twenty bags for a refill.

At the shopping center on the outskirts of Cold Harbor, the company had two machines. They had been checked three times each on the Fourth of July. More bags of ice had been added each time. "In other words, none of the machines was allowed to run out of ice," Heimrich said.

"They're firm about that, M.L. They regard it as a public service. 'Does the power company run out of electricity?' Way the guy I talked to put it."

"And you told him, yes, every now and then, I suppose?"

"Didn't think of it, M.L. Just thanked him and hung up. They were cooperative, I'll say that."

Heimrich agreed they had been. Probably had to go and nudge awake their computer; ice venders' computers probably hibernate during winter months.

Heimrich stood up. He said, "Looks as if we'll have to badger Mrs. Lord again, doesn't it, Charlie? And her son, who'd rather be called Nolan."

The sun was bright outside the barracks, and it was warming things up a little. The temperature was above zero—five above. The wind had died down a little. There was almost no ice left on the roads. As, driving south on N.Y. 11-F, they approached Hawthorne Drive, Forniss slowed down, and set the blinker for a right turn.

But Heimrich said, "No, Charlie. Let's go on down to Cold Harbor first. Talk to a barber. Maybe a couple of barbers."

Forniss switched off the direction indicator and continued down 11-F. A car, running too close behind them, blared indignation at this change of mind, and passed, still grumbling angrily. It shot ahead. "Ten over the limit," Forniss said. "At least ten, maybe twenty."

"At least twenty," Heimrich said. "But we're after bigger game, aren't we?"

In Cold Harbor, 11-F became Main Street. There were two barber shops on Main Street. Forniss pulled up at the first. They went in. There were four chairs in the shop, but only one barber. He was running clippers over the head of a plump man in his late sixties or early seventies. It was obvious that he had given up on hair; the barber was clipping him bald.

Reaction to the present trend, Heimrich supposed, not without sympathy. The three unattended chairs represented the trend.

The barber said, "Good morning. Be with you right away."

There was a row of chairs along the wall of the shop. Nobody was sitting in any of them. Heimrich and Forniss sat and waited. The barber zipped the last of the stubble off the man's plump head and whisked off the cloth covering him. He brushed the plump man carefully and took two dollar bills from him and said, "Thank

174

you, sir." The plump man went out of the shop and the barber said, "Every week he comes in. Before it gets a quarter of an inch long." He smiled a welcome at Heimrich and Forniss but looked a little surprised when they both stood up.

"Just a couple of questions," Heimrich said. "A young man named Lord one of your customers?"

"Mr. Alan Lord?"

"That's the man, Mr. Barnes."

"BOB BARNES BARBER SHOP" was what it said on the window.

"Not Barnes," the barber said. "Been dead for years, old Bob has. I'm Nat Curtis. Yes, the Lord kid comes in every couple of weeks. When he's around, that is. Way his father used to do. Burton Lord, his father was. He's dead too. Some woman shot him at a picnic they were having. Used to produce plays, the old man did. What I hear, anyway. Had a good head of hair, Mr. Lord did. And sort of particular about the way it was cut. Remember one time——"

"Yes, Mr. Curtis," Heimrich said. "About young Mr. Lord. He's been coming in for some time?"

"Six months, maybe. Usually Mondays. Tuesdays sometimes, though. What's all this about young Mr. Lord?"

"State police," Heimrich said. "Inspector Heimrich. Just checking up on something."

"Law now against getting your hair cut, Inspector? Damn if it don't look like there is sometimes. One law the kids seem to obey, damn it to hell." He scowled at the unattended chairs. "Few years ago there were three of us here, and not more than keeping up. Four on Saturdays. Now, hell, I twiddle my thumbs half the time. Morning, Mr. Isaacs. Be right with you."

The last was to a tall man with a good deal of black hair who had just come into the shop. The man said, "Morning, Nat." He sat down on one of the chairs and picked up a magazine. The magazine was *Popular Mechanics*.

"It's still legal to get your hair cut," Heimrich said, looking at his own in the mirror. By his standards, it could stand cutting. By Susan's, it was already too short. Susan's view prevailed, within reason, of course. "Probably just a fad, this long-hair business, Mr. Curtis. Probably it'll pass."

"Hope it does before I do," Nat Curtis said. "Used to be barbering was pretty solid. Like undertaking, almost. Sooner or later, know what I mean? Sooner or later, everybody——"

"Yes, Mr. Curtis, I know what you mean. To get back to Alan Lord. Been coming in about six months, you say. Starting, say, in July?"

"Somewheres around there. Hey, wait a minute. Last summer the Fourth came on a Thursday, way I remember. What I did, I closed the shop Tuesday, not open Wednesday, anyhow, and took myself a little vacation. Went fishing. Man I know's got a little lake. Keeps it stocked with bass. You pay him by the pound you catch. Pretty good luck I had, too. One of them weighed close to four pounds. Gave me quite a fight, that one did. While there, thought I'd lost him."

Heimrich waited for what he was pretty sure was coming.

"About this long, that one was," Curtis said, holding his hands apart to demonstrate—holding them wide apart. He could have been measuring a good-sized salmon.

"Quite a bass," Heimrich said. "Alan Lord came in for the first time after you reopened the shop, Mr. Curtis?"

"That's right. Monday the eighth of July that would have been. Probably wonder how I remember so good, don't you?"

"How do you, Mr. Curtis?"

"On account, could have been the first haircut he ever had. From the looks of it, that is. Yellow hair, damn near down to his shoulders. First came in, I thought he was a girl. About to tell him I didn't cut women's hair. Then I saw him from in front, know what I mean?"

"Yes, Mr. Curtis, I get the point. Tell you why he'd decided to—to change his style?"

"Said it was too hot. Also fell over his eyes, as it sure as hell must have. Wanted it good and short. Ended up my giving him a brush cut, damn near. Nice-looking boy he turned out to be after we'd got rid of all that hair."

"And he's been coming in every two weeks since?"

"Pretty much. Oh, he missed a couple of times in late August. He and his mother went away some place before he went back to this college of his. But he's kept on getting it cut up there, wherever it is."

"Cornell, I think, Mr. Curtis. Up in Ithaca, that is."

"Wherever you say, Inspector. In last Monday for a cut. Made it before we got all that ice. Can't say much for the barber he's been going to up at this Cornell place. Not much good around the ears. Anyway, I fixed him up for Christmas. Going into the city to see his father, he told me. Suppose they've got old Lord stuffed or something?"

"Burton Lord was his stepfather, Mr. Curtis. His real father's named Nolan. He lives in New York."

"Divorced from his mother, that would be? Hell of a lot of people getting divorces these days. Don't know as I hold with it myself. Course, I've never been married. You married, Inspector?"

"Yes," Heimrich said. "I'm married, Mr. Curtis. And thanks for sparing us your time."

"Only," Curtis said, "I still don't know what it's all about, do I?"

"No, Mr. Curtis, you don't, do you? Thanks again."

As he and Forniss went out of the shop, Nat Curtis was tucking Mr. Isaacs in around the neck. Curtis was talking; Isaacs appeared to be looking abstractedly into the distance.

In the car, Forniss raised his eyebrows.

"Yes, Charlie," Heimrich said, "I guess it's time to go badger people."

"Peters is going to be sore as hell," Forniss said, as he U-turned in Main Street.

"Yes, Charlie," Heimrich said, "I'm afraid the District Attorney's not going to like us much."

Chapter 14

THE THREE-CAR GARAGE was twenty yards or so down the driveway from the Lord house. A somewhat battered small car, well along in years, stood in front of the garage. Forniss pulled the police car up beside it and cut the motor.

The garage faced south. All three doors were open, and sunlight poured into the garage. There were two cars in the garage, the sports model Mercedes Alan Lord had been driving the night before and a Cadillac. The third space was empty except for a bicycle against the forewall. A big man was sweeping the garage with a push broom. The man wore a heavy coat, fleece-lined, and a cap with earflaps. The flaps were down over his ears and, when they first saw him, he was half behind the Cadillac, using his broom. He came out and faced them and began, slowly, to sweep toward them. He had scattered sawdust on the floor and swept a pile of it toward the front of the garage.

Heimrich said, "Morning." There was no evidence that the sweeper heard him or indeed, that he saw them. Heimrich repeated himself, more loudly. The man pushed the earflap up from his right ear and said, "Huh?"

"I just said good morning," Heimrich told him. The man—a very big man, probably somewhere around sixty—said, "O.K.," and reached toward the earflap, evidently to pull it down again, conversation finished.

"And a damned cold one," Heimrich said.

Instead of covering his right ear, the man uncovered his left. He told Heimrich he could say that again.

"Damned cold for garage sweeping," Heimrich said.

"Yeah," the man said. "Sure is, mister. Way they want it. The kid, anyway. The young squirt, between us, mister. Wants I should call him Mr. Alan. Says that's what people who work here always call him. Well, I work here. Sort of, anyway."

He returned to pushing his broom, adding to the ripple of sawdust. He did not, however, re-cover his ears.

"Sort of?"

"Couple of days a week. In the winter, that is. What they call a yardman. Odds and ends mostly, except when it snows. Then I plow the drive. Summers they've got what they call a gardener. Comes on in the early spring he does. Mows the lawn and weeds the flower beds. What they tell me, anyhow."

He pulled the left earflap down and reached toward the right. He changed his mind in midreach.

"Fritz Krippendorf, they calls him," he said. "Foreigner of some sort, sounds like. Drives the car sometimes for Mrs. Lord. Used to live up there."

He pointed toward the roof of the garage. Heimrich had seen the outside staircase in the garage wall which led, obviously, to an apartment above it.

"Where Mr. Alan stays now," the man said, and pulled the right flap. He put fairly derisive quotation marks around "Mr. Alan."

He began to sweep again, more vigorously than before.

His broom hit something on the cement floor. What he had hit came out of the sawdust and skittered across the cement. It made a metallic sound as it skidded on the cement. It came out of the garage onto the gravel Heimrich and Forniss stood on and stopped near Forniss's feet. A small tool, possibly, Heimrich thought, and watched Forniss stoop to pick it up.

Forniss looked at the metal object and handed it to Heimrich. It was not a forgotten tool. It was a thin piece of worn metal—worn, evidently, much thinner than it had once been. Anonymous metal, at first sight.

But maybe not. Maybe part of the broken crosspiece of a tire chain; a piece worn almost through by pounding on road surfaces which were not snow-covered. Heimrich looked at Forniss, who nodded his head. Heimrich put the sliver of metal in his pocket.

They left the burly man sweeping and walked toward the house.

"A good many cars drip oil, don't they?" Forniss said. "Old cars especially. Leak where they've been standing."

Heimrich agreed that old cars sometimes leaked oil where they had been standing. He pressed the bell at the front door of the big house of the late Burton Lord and, of course, of the present Amelia Lord and, part time at any rate, of her son Alan. Who, when he was not away at school, occupied the apartment above the garage, where a foreigner named Fritz Krippendorf once had spent his off-duty hours. What it sounded like, anyway.

Didn't need to mean anything, of course. The young like to get away from family, have a place of their own. Convenient, of course, to a food supply. A place to entertain friends, away from parental supervision. And, come to that, a place to be away from parents. Or from one parent? Perhaps an adoptive parent?

The small old man in the neat dark suit opened the door for them. (Heimrich couldn't at the moment remember his name. Getting old and memory fading.)

Mrs. Lord was in her rooms. She seldom came down much before noon. Mr. Alan was, he thought, in the library reading. Well, it was a bad hour. But he could ask, if the Inspector insisted.

Heimrich was sorry that the time was inconvenient, but he would still like to see Mrs. Lord and her son. He would try not to take up too much of their time. The man in the dark suit said he would see, and if the Inspector and the other gentleman would care to wait in the drawing room?

Carson. That was the butler's name. He showed them into the big living room. In the fireplace, flames were licking at heavy logs. The logs were symmetrical, and all much of a size. They looked, somehow, like part of a stage set, but they were real. They were really giving off heat. The big room was warm. Very comfortingly warm to men just in from the frigid out-of-doors. Probably get too warm if they had to stay in it long.

Yes, Carson could take their coats. He helped them off with their coats, although he was a small man to help men so big. He carried the coats away.

"Sawdust doesn't really get rid of oil stains," Forniss said. "Just smears them up."

Heimrich said, "That's true, Charlie," and they both sat down, not too far from the fire. They sat for almost five minutes and then Carson came back. He said that Mrs. Lord would see them and was coming down. He said he would go and tell Mr. Alan that the Inspector would like to see him.

He didn't need to. Alan Lord came in by a door at the far end of the long room. He was wearing a yellow sports shirt, long-sleeved as accorded with the weather outside, and dark slacks. He spoke as he walked toward them.

"You said you wouldn't bother us anymore," he said. There was stridency in his voice.

"Said I hoped I wouldn't need to," Heimrich said. "But one or two things have come up."

"So you're going to bother my mother again," Alan Lord said. "You may as well know, I'm going to stick around while you do. Whether you want me to or not."

"Oh, we want you to," Heimrich said. "Your mother's on the way down, Mr. Lord. We'll wait for her, shall we?"

"I suppose you're going to say the District Attorney sent you," the boy said.

He is a boy, Heimrich thought. At the moment a petulant boy. He said, "Just sit down, son. Your mother shouldn't be long."

Alan Lord sat down, near the fire. He scowled. But then his face lighted up as Amelia Lord came into the room from the entrance foyer. He said, "Good morning, Mother. These men are——"

"Yes, dear," Amelia said. "I see the Inspector and Lieutenant Forniss are here again. What is it this time, Inspector? More questions from Mr. Peters to make sure what I'm going to say at the trial? We've been over all that, haven't we? And I'm quite clear in my mind about all of it."

Heimrich was sure she was. However, one or two points had come up.

He and Forniss were both standing, now; looking down at mother and son.

"One of them is this," Heimrich said. He took the sliver of metal out of his pocket. He held it out toward Alan Lord, who took it. The boy looked at it and turned it over in his hands. Then he looked up at Heimrich and shook his head.

"Doesn't mean anything to you?" Heimrich said. "No idea what it could be?"

"No. Just a little piece of iron. Steel, maybe."

"Or where we might have found it?"

Alan merely shook his head at that one.

"It may be a broken piece of tire chain," Heimrich told him. "The yardman swept it up on your garage floor just now. Says you told him to sweep out the garage today, Alan. Pretty cold day for that, I'd think."

"Quigley does outdoor work for us, Inspector. Isn't much for him to do this time of year." That was Amelia Lord. "And in the garage he'd be sheltered," she added. "They say it's very cold and windy out. Alan was quite right to give him a job under shelter."

"I suppose so," Heimrich said. "You use chains on the Cadillac, Mrs. Lord? Or on the Mercedes?"

"I don't think so. My son takes care of that sort of thing. Now that Burton isn't around to do it. Do we ever use chains, Alan?" He did not appear to hear her. He was gazing into the fire. She said "Alan?" again, this time more sharply.

"No, Mother," the boy said. "People don't so much nowadays. Snow tires are much better than they used to be. They put steel studs in them nowadays." He looked up at Heimrich. He held the strip of metal out and Heimrich bent down and took it from him. Heimrich scrutinized it, turning it over in his fingers. He nodded his head, presumably at what he saw, then he put the metal strip back in his pocket.

"You don't know it's off a tire chain," Alan Lord said. "And I don't know how it got in our garage, if it did, like you say."

"It is a little hard to identify," Heimrich said. "But it was on the garage floor. The yardman saw it. Saw Lieutenant Forniss pick it up. We'll have the lab boys check on it."

"Is that all you came for, Inspector?" Mrs. Lord asked. "Just to show my son a piece of scrap metal?"

"No, Mrs. Lord. Not quite all. Before Mr. Kemper died, were you and your husband at all friendly with the Kempers? Being close neighbors, as you were?"

"We knew them. The way neighbors get to know one another in the country. Only casually, however. And several years ago. Not recently. Not my son and I, that is. Not since Tony Kemper died so suddenly."

"Did you ever go to their house, Mrs. Lord?"

"A few times, perhaps. For drinks, and things like that. Of course, Alan—"

She stopped. Stopped a little abruptly, Heimrich thought. She looked at her son.

"What Mother means, Inspector," Alan said. "Two or three years ago, I used to use their pool sometimes. They asked me to. It was while they were still putting ours in, you see."

"The Kemper pool is beyond their house," Heimrich said. "From here, I mean."

"Yes, Inspector," Amelia said. "Where that woman says she was when my husband was shot. When she shot him."

"That's where she says she was," Heimrich agreed. "Alan, when you were using the pool, after you'd used it, did Mrs. Kemper ever invite you into the house? For a Coke, say? Or a glass of iced tea, say? Because probably they were hot days when you used to use the pool. Sometimes, as you say."

"Once or twice, I guess. I didn't know about her and—and my stepfather then, of course."

Heimrich said he saw. He said, "By the way, when you went over to use the pool, how did you go? I mean, did you walk across the field or drive over?"

"Drove, mostly. Like you say, it was usually hot weather."

"And went in through the house? And then out to the pool?"

"Not mostly. Once or twice, maybe."

"Really, Inspector," Mrs. Lord said. "What is the point of all this? All this triviality? My son used the pool over there a few times. Before I found out that that woman and my husband were sleeping together. Not afterward, I assure you."

"You told him about this affair?"

"Yes. I thought he ought to know. My son and I don't keep things from each other. To get back. What possible difference can it make how Alan got to that pool of theirs?"

"Probably none," Heimrich said. "Another thing that's probably trivial. You used to wear your hair quite long, my son tells me. When did you——"

"Your stepson," Alan said. "He wouldn't want you to call him your son."

"No?" Heimrich said. "He's never said so. Never indicated he minded. When did you decide to have your hair cut, Alan?"

"For God's sake, mister. Some time last summer, I guess. Before I went back to college, anyway. Because it got too hot. The guys at college kidded me about it a good deal. Said I'd turned out square. That sort of thing."

"Just because it was too hot? Long hair was too hot?"

"Well, it annoyed the old man, wearing my hair long. Mr. Lord, I mean. Of course, everything about me annoyed him. Just my being around annoyed him."

"Alan," his mother said, "you oughtn't to say things like that. It isn't true, Inspector. Burton was very fond of Alan, really. After all, he was the one who insisted on adopting him."

"He wanted me to be called Lord, is all. Lord of the manor or something. Carry on the name. Even if it isn't mine to carry. If he was so fond of me, why did he have me move out to the garage apartment? The chauffeur's apartment, really. Just so I wouldn't be in his hair so much. That was why, wasn't it?"

"No, dear," his mother said. "He suggested you move out there because he thought you'd like a place of your own."

"Yeah," Alan said. "Away from you. So I wouldn't be around to remind you of my real father. So there wouldn't be a Nolan around. Why he changed my name, wasn't it? When I was too young to know the difference. What he thought, anyway. Not that he'd have given a damn. And because I look like my father. Just shut the Nolans out altogether, and he knew it. That's the way it was, and you know it, Mother."

Amelia Lord answered this with a sigh. A somewhat theatrical sigh, Heimrich thought. Then she said, "Really, dear. The Inspector isn't interested in all this. In your strange notions about Burton. Why should he be?"

Alan didn't answer that. He merely shrugged his shoulders. It was going to dead-end there, Heimrich thought. Which was a pity.

"You got your hair cut short just after the Fourth of July, Alan," Heimrich said. "According to your barber, anyway. Way you remember it?"

"Could be. Sometime last summer, like I said."

"Speaking of the Fourth, Alan. You were out getting ice when your stepfather was shot. That's right, isn't it? What you told me? Had to go clear into Cold Harbor for it, because the two nearer places had run out?"

"Sure. Like I told you."

"Yes," Heimrich said. "I was pretty sure that was what you told me. Only there's a catch in it, boy. There was plenty of ice in the machine at the Gulf station. And at the Sunoco station down the road. You see, both machines had been refilled early that afternoon, because it was such a hot day and there was so much demand for ice. So why did you lie about where you were, Alan? Because you wanted to show you weren't some other place?"

"Inspector," Amelia Lord said. "You don't—" But then she stopped speaking, and her face seemed to fall apart as she looked at her son.

His smooth young face did not seem to change.

"He had it coming," Alan Lord said. His voice was steady. He looked not at Heimrich or his mother, but at the fire. "He did Mother dirt with that trashy woman. She should never have left my father. Now she's free to go back to him, isn't she? Now they can get married again, can't they? And we can all be together, the way we ought to be."

Nobody answered his questions. Amelia Lord got up from her chair and walked out of the room. She walked like an old woman.

Alan turned in his chair. He watched his mother walk out of the room. He looked like a small boy, Heimrich thought—a small boy who was about to start crying.

Chapter 15

IT WAS a little after six when Heimrich ran the Buick into the garage. It was still cold, but the wind had died down and stars were out. The house was warm and the fire burning. And lights glowed and twinkled on the Christmas tree. Susan was in the kitchen, and she said, "Hi, darling," and looked up at him. "So it's finished," she said, although he had not told her anything. He kissed her and said, "Yes, wrapped up, dear. All over but the shouting."

"I could tell from your face," Susan said. "Your face tells a lot, when you let it. But the shouting? You don't look in a shouting mood. It was the boy?"

"You're a good guesser," he told her. "Yes, the boy. And I'm not doing the shouting. District Attorney Peters will take care of that, when I tell him he didn't see what he thought he saw, told the grand jury he saw. Yes, the boy's confessed. He wanted to sign it Alan Nolan. Said he's through being a Lord. We told him he had to sign his legal name. That he could apply later to the courts to have it changed."

He looked down at her.

"Yes," Susan said, "I could too, Merton. Go sit by the fire. I'll make them."

Heimrich went and sat by the fire. Susan made the drinks.

"Two murders," Heimrich told her, as they raised their glasses.

"His stepfather, and then Sam. He's a weirdo, as Michael said he was. Seems to feel that both killings were entirely—well, logical. Understandable. Lord was an intruder: it was as if he had shot somebody who was breaking into a house. And Sam—he seems to think that was self-defense. It was this way—"

Briefly, he told her how it had been. When he had finished, she looked at the fire for a time. Then she said, "I think we could both do with another drink," and went to get them. When she brought them back, she said, "Michael ought to be back almost any time now, if there's a cab."

Heimrich said, "A cab?"

"At the station. For the six forty-two. From New York, dear."

Heimrich knew where the six forty-two came from, usually at about seven. He didn't, offhand, know why Michael Faye would be on it.

"Mr. Purvis brought Joan's car up this morning," Susan said. "Not long after you left. She said she would drive on into the city, and her father, and Michael said, not without him she wouldn't. And—well, she didn't make any fuss about that, and they went off. Around ten, I'd say."

"Didn't want to leave her unprotected," Heimrich said.

"I suppose so. Or—didn't want to leave her, period. I think they're both pretty serious about it, Merton. Dead serious." She shook her head at herself. She had not meant to say "dead." Merton Heimrich does not need to be reminded of death.

"Yes," Heimrich said. "I think they are, dear. You don't mind?"

"Mind? Why should I mind, dear?"

"You're his mother, Susan. I thought mothers were supposed to mind. Young leaving the nest. Mothers mourning."

"We don't run a nest, Heimrich." She calls him by his last name when he is being obtuse, and she is a little annoyed. "Our son is grown up. He—" She stopped, because car lights shone through the glass of the front door.

"Speaking of our son," she said, and went to open the door for him. She switched on the floodlight.

But the car, instead of backing for a turn and a trip back to the

Van Brunt station, was going into the Heimrich garage. And it was a red Volkswagen. Susan left the front door and went, instead, to open the kitchen door.

"It's me again," Joan Collins said.

Michael, carrying a suitcase in either hand, spoke from behind her. "It's us, she means," he said.

"Only," Joan said, "I wanted him to drop me off at the inn. Only he wouldn't."

"The inn," Michael said, "isn't a safe place for her. So—well, I just brought her home. I don't mind the sofa at all."

"My father," Joan said, "had to go to Miami this afternoon. On business, he said. He said we could stay in the apartment. After we told him, that is. But Michael wanted to bring me back here. But I do think I really ought to stay at the inn. And——"

"No inn," Susan said. "Told him what, dear?"

"Why," Joan said, "that we're going to get married. We only decided that while we were driving in this morning. Michael convinced me we might as well. And we really haven't anything against marriage. At least, I guess we haven't. I hope you don't mind, Susan."

Susan smiled at the long-haired girl. She put an arm about her tall son, and took Joan's hand in her own free hand.

Heimrich, standing with his back to the fire, said, "I think this rates a drink, my dears."

"And," Susan said, "steaks. I'll start water running on them."

Joan went out to the kitchen to help turn on the water. Heimrich went out to the breezeway to get the charcoal started.

It was a little after eight when Heimrich woke up the next morning. Nobody else woke up. Susan slept peacefully in her bed. Michael, although he had brought blankets and a pillow out for the sofa, was not sleeping on the sofa. Heimrich had not really supposed he would be. Heimrich drank orange juice while the coffee dripped; he soft-boiled an egg and toasted a slice of bread. The fire had died down behind its screen during the night. He did not rebuild it. With the house comfortably warm, fire would be for the evening.

Heimrich called the barracks and told the duty sergeant what he

wanted done. He was about to go out for the Buick when Susan
came into the living room. She said, a little dreamily, that it had
been quite a party. She added, "Our son doesn't get engaged every
day, of course. Is there coffee?"

Merton Heimrich assured her there was coffee. He put on his
heavy coat while she got her coffee. When she came back she
looked at the sofa. "Apparently Michael didn't sleep there last
night," she said.

"Did you expect him to, dear?"

"No, Merton. You're off to the barracks?"

"Carmel," Heimrich told her. "To listen to Mr. Peters shouting."

She said, "Be careful," but not what he should be careful of.

The Buick was not enthusiastic about starting, but it was not as
stubborn as it had been the day before. The weather was not as
stubborn, either. It was a sunny day and a windless one. Up to the
low twenties, Heimrich guessed it was. Might reach up to freezing
by midday.

He was in the outer office of District Attorney Jonathan Peters
at ten o'clock, the time of the appointment the duty sergeant had
made for him. At ten twenty-five he was told that Mr. Peters
would see him now.

"Sit down, Heimrich," Peters said. He sounded grumpy; he
looked grumpy. "Understand you've been meddling."

"Discharging my duty as a police officer," Heimrich said. "And
getting a confession to murder. To two murders. You mind, Counselor?"

It was clear from his expression that Peters did mind.

"And," Heimrich told him, "here's a copy of the boy's confession. All according to Hoyle. Duly signed, with the kid's legal
name. Ready for the next session of the grand jury. Same one that
indicted Mrs. Kemper?"

"No. New panel. Session starts in February. Damn it, man, I
saw her shoot him."

"Saw somebody," Heimrich said. "Somebody wearing dark
slacks and a yellow shirt. Somebody with long hair. It was a hazy
day, Counselor. Anybody could have made a mistake. Seen what

he was expected to see. Only it was Alan Lord, not Loren Kemper. Roughly the same size, the two of them. But not the same shape. Which was what Sam Jackson saw and took a picture of. And died because of. All in here, Mr. Peters." He slid the copy of Alan Lord's confession across Peters's desk.

Peters looked at it. He did not immediately pick it up.

"All right," Heimrich said, "I'll tell you about it, if you'd rather. Although it's all there. A little rambling and self-justifying, but all there. Young Lord didn't like his stepfather. Thought he had broken up the marriage of his mother and his real father. As probably he did. We haven't checked that out yet. And then Lord had this affair with Mrs. Kemper and got caught at it. 'He was unfaithful to my mother,' way the boy puts it. A traditionalist of sorts, the kid is. Lord was an intruder, between his father and his mother. And between his mother and himself, come to that. He doesn't quite realize that part of it, I think. Oedipus creeps in.

"Also, with Burton Lord out of the way, his father and mother could remarry. And the three of them could be together, as he thought they ought to be."

"His mother go along with that?" Peters asked. He picked the confession up. He did not unfold it.

"She says not. Says it was the wild idea of the poor, dear, foolish boy. Just something in his head, she says it was. Very upset, Mrs. Lord is."

"You expect her not to be, Inspector?"

"No. And I expect she's been carrying it around in her mind for months. You see, the ice he finally brought back had begun to drip. She admits she noticed that, and that it worried her a little. The bags they use keep the cubes frozen for quite a while."

"What's this about ice?"

Heimrich told him about the ice; about Alan Lord's assertion he had had trouble finding ice, so explaining his prolonged absence from the party. "Plenty of ice five minutes away, Counselor. We've checked on that."

Alan had used the time to stop by the Kemper house and get Loren Kemper's rifle out of the hall closet—"he'd been in the house before, knew where the rifle was"—and killed his stepfather. "Left her rifle to be found and identified. Took off over the field at a dead run, apparently for the house. Actually, for his car. It's all there, Mr. Peters. Right in front of you."

"You say he killed Jackson too?"

"What he says. All in his confession. Says Jackson called him up —after Jackson had looked at the film, presumably—and told him he had a picture he thought Alan ought to see. The film shows it was a male running, not a female. Jackson had his suspicions. Probably nothing more. The face doesn't show in the picture. Jackson, at a guess, merely wanted to give young Lord a jolt. Break him down."

"Tampering with a witness, Jackson was doing, Inspector."

"Witness to what, Counselor? If Mrs. Kemper had killed Lord, young Lord wasn't there. Off getting ice. Would you have called him, Mr. Peters?"

"Possibly. Not about the actual shooting. So Jackson said he had this picture?"

"Way Alan tells it. And thought it was a picture of him shooting his stepfather. An identifiable picture. It isn't. Just a picture of someone with long hair rubbing something in the grass. And of a male running. Not the threat the boy thought it was. But he didn't know that. He did know the picture wouldn't be admissible without Jackson to identify it. Right on that, wasn't he?"

"Probably. So he ran Jackson down with a stolen station wagon."

"Borrowed, he calls it. Says he'd been down to Van Brunt that day to see a friend. Rode his bicycle because it looked as if it was going to be a nice day. It started out like that, you remember. And the forecast was for partly cloudy and turning colder. Didn't work out quite that way, you'll remember."

"Sure as hell didn't."

The cold rain had set in as Alan had started to pedal home. It was raining hard when he reached Father Armstrong's church, and saw the station wagon standing in front of it. He cycled up and found the ignition key was still in the lock. There didn't, he says, seem to be anybody in the church, so he decided to borrow the wagon to get home. Put his bicycle in it and drove home. "Says it wasn't until later that he decided to use the wagon to kill Jackson. Admits he telephoned Jackson's office to find out whether Jackson was going to the inn for dinner. He'd been asking around about Jackson. Finding out what he could about Jackson's habits.

"So—he parked at the inn and waited for Jackson to come out. Saw us go in with Michael and Michael's girl. Saw the light go on in a window above the parking lot and somebody looking out of it. Figured, rightly, that it was the girl he'd seen with Michael, whom he knows slightly. Figured, wrongly, that she could identify the driver of the wagon. So the next morning he drove back to Van Brunt and parked where he could see Miss Collins drive out on 11-F if she was going to. She did. Dropped my son off at the inn. He followed her. He forced her off the road at a convenient place. Didn't kill her. Didn't even damage her much. Had another try at it, from the field next my house. Used his rifle this time. Missed again. Oh, he ditched the station wagon off Jackson's drive after he brushed the Volks. Not, he says, trying to implicate Jackson's houseman, Friday. Says he'd never heard of Friday. Just seemed like a good place to hide the wagon. Still had his bicycle in the wagon, and rode home on it. So there it is, Counselor. All right there in front of you."

Now, finally, District Attorney Jonathan Peters picked up the copy of Alan Lord's confession and unfolded it and began to read. Heimrich waited. Peters read fast. After only a few minutes he looked up. He seemed surprised to find Inspector Heimrich still there. He said, "All you've got, Inspector?"

"Enough, I'd think. Oh, a piece of metal off a broken tire chain. Lab report on some paint scrapings. All yours when you're ready, Counselor. You'll get the indictment against Mrs. Kemper dismissed? And turn her loose?"

"Looks like I'll have to," Peters said. He was still grumpy about it. A man couldn't believe the evidence of his own two eyes. Even eyes with twenty-twenty vision. And, of course, he'd have to admit it. Wouldn't look so good next fall, when election time came around.

Merton Heimrich didn't go to the barracks. If somebody else murdered somebody else, they would let him know. Meanwhile, he'd take the day off. Get a little time with his own stepson and the stepson's girl. And, as went without thinking, with Susan.